ALPHA KNIGHT

RENEE ROSE

Published in the United States of America

Renee Rose Romance

Editor: Simone Elise

WANT FREE RENEE ROSE BOOKS?

Go to http://subscribepage.com/alphastemp to sign up for Renee Rose's newsletter and receive a free copy of *Theirs to Protect, Owned by the Marine, Theirs to Punish, The Alpha's Punishment, Disobedience at the Dressmaker's* and *Her Billionaire Boss.* In addition to the free stories, you will also get special pricing, exclusive previews and news of new releases.

USA TODAY BESTSELLING AUTHORS
Alpha's
TEMPTATION
A billionaire werewolf romance
RENEE ROSE & LEE SAVINO

PROLOGUE

o

On the day everything goes to shit, you don't wake up thinking, *Today my whole life changes.*

It wasn't like that the day the two service members showed up at our door when I was eight to give my mom the news Dad's helicopter got shot down in Yemen. And it wasn't like that today.

Today was like any day. I woke up, showered, went to school, stayed after for football practice, same as ever.

I never expected the screech of tires as Sheriff Gleason skids to a stop in the parking lot by the field. Didn't foresee him marching out with his hands on his hips like he's about to arrest one of us.

Coach Jamison jogs over to meet him on the edge, his body rigid with alert.

And then they both turn their heads and look at me.

"Fenton!" Coach's voice booms. His alpha wolf authority ripples through me, all the way to my shoes.

Fuck.

What did I do?

I whip off my helmet and stalk over like I'm pissed about the interruption, but it's just my wolf rearing up to face perceived danger. There's no *flight* in the *fight or flight* for an alpha male—especially not in a teen wolf who doesn't always have aggression under control.

"Get in the car," Sheriff Gleason snarls.

"Why?" I demand.

Coach's hand drops on my nape, above the shoulder pads. His fingers tighten in warning. If it were anyone else, I'd already have him on his fucking back, but Coach is like a god to us. A better father figure than most of us have and always, *always* in our corner.

I turn to look at him searchingly.

"It's Winslow," he says because he's not a dick like the sheriff, keeping me in the dark.

Winslow—my older brother.

"Fuck."

Coach doesn't call me on the language violation, which tells me this is as bad as I'm thinking.

And then I know exactly what it's about.

Or at least I think I do.

Because I saw this shit coming way back when it started.

The only question is, *what do they want from me?*

CHAPTER 1

Six Weeks Earlier

loane

STEALING the 2016 Porsche 911 is the easy part. At least it's the fun part. This is only my second car theft, but I think I have a real gift for it.

I'm dressed as daddy's spoiled princess in a pair of Rag & Bone skinny jeans with wedge heels and a Balmain cropped tee. All remnants of my past life, when I really was daddy's spoiled princess. When stealing a car meant lifting a pair of keys out of my dad's lock box and choosing one of the twelve sports cars in his garage.

My hair is pulled up in a twist, and I have a khaki rhinestone ball cap pulled over my eyes to hide my face. Anyone who glances over in this crowded parking lot will see someone who matches the car.

It's just a matter of finding the right make and model in a location without camera surveillance. I've been walking around the Scottsdale mall parking lot for days now, dodging cameras and mall cops.

Finally, I spot one. A blue Porsche 911 Carrera 4 GTS, and it looks to be full leather interior. *MSRP* can range from 100k to 200k depending on the engine and gadgets inside. I know because my father had one just like it sitting in our garage before... before the fall. Before everything went to shit. Before I had to learn how to poach pretty cars out of mall parking lots.

In theory, ordinary cars are best—the kind that blend in. But I don't have the luxury of time or lower risk. I'm on a payment schedule with dangerous people, and the Porsche will bring in big bucks.

So the Porsche it is. I already bought a totalled version at the salvage yard, so I have a salvage title. Now all I have to do is swap some parts out, including the VIN, and retitle this baby to sell.

Unfortunately, that means trusting a chop shop to do the swapping and cutting them in on half the proceeds because I don't have the skills.

Yet.

I plan to learn. In fact, I think I'll see if the guy can teach me on this one, so the next car I can do on my own.

I walk up to the car like I own the place. Like I own the Porsche, I mean.

Like I own the house and job or father or husband that match this car. It's a role I know intimately. Lived my whole life. Entitled. Cosseted. Spoiled.

Daddy's little girl has fallen far from grace.

My device does its work, and the locks pop. Another

few seconds and the car revs, and then I'm driving wild and free.

Out of the parking lot. Onto the highway.

Up to Wolf Ridge, the weird-ass community just past Cave Hills.

Right where I landed when my dad went to jail.

Bo

I RIDE my 1984 Triumph to the shop after football practice because we've been slammed, and my brother and uncle need me around more than just on the weekends.

Plus, my best friend Cole's been no-showing for work lately. I don't know what the fuck his problem is, but I'm not gonna bust his balls considering the shit he's been dealing with at home this semester.

I'm starving, which makes me cranky as hell.

But I forget all about the hunger because… *hot damn.*

The first thing I see is her ass. Fuck-hot-amazing ass in tight jeans that show every curve of her muscular cheeks. And looooong fucking legs punctated by platform heels that lift everything.

I give a silent hooty-hoo whistle in my head in appreciation.

She's leaning over the engine of an electric blue 2016 Porsche. My brother Winslow is beside her, pointing something out.

At first, I assume she's a shifter, like most everyone in Wolf Ridge and try to figure out who she can be.

Then I catch her scent.

Human.

Human who should've been a shifter. Because she's built like a she-wolf. Tall. Big-boned. Sturdy, athletic. She didn't get those lean muscular legs lying around on her bed playing on her phone.

No, she works for them.

And—holy hell—when she lifts her torso and turns, my dick gets hard. Because she's young. Maybe my age. And beautiful. Caramel-colored hair with reddish highlights, copper eyes that match, and a beauty mark that makes her look like an old-fashioned movie star.

I want to fuck her right up against that 911. Then I see the logo stretching across the front of her tits. *Cave Hills Cross Country.*

That explains the legs. And the expensive car. Looks like someone wrecked Daddy's ride and brought it up here to get it fixed before he finds out.

Maybe because I'm hangry or maybe because she got my dick hard and I know I can't have her, but I take an instant dislike to her. Fucking Cave Hills spoiled little rich bitch. Cave Hills kids only come to Wolf Ridge when they're looking for trouble. And this girl is definitely trouble.

Winslow catches sight of me. He stops what he's saying to level me a *what-the-fuck-do-you-want?* look.

And that's when I know something's off.

Because he wouldn't use that expression because I interrupted him with this chick. He wouldn't be hot for a human girl—Winslow hates humans.

Which means he wants me to stay away for some other reason.

"Don't you have a door to replace on that VW?" he jerks his thumb toward the other bay. We were waiting for the new part to be delivered, and the VW was his project, not mine. Now I'm certain he's trying to get rid of me.

"Yeah. Okay." I still don't move.

Prickles raise on the back of my neck. I look at the Porsche again. Maybe it's not her daddy's ride. What were they looking at under the hood?

Unease washes over me. It's a familiar warning—the kind I get every time my big brother is about to do something really stupid. Or dangerous. Something I'm gonna have to try to talk him out of or stop.

Fuck.

Please tell me it's not a stolen vehicle, and he's about to help this girl fence it.

When I don't move, Winslow's lip curls, and his eyes flash yellow. The wolf in me experiences the threat viscerally.

I have no choice but to drop my gaze and lift my chin, showing my throat. My brother has a mean streak, and he's dangerous as hell, even though we're family. I toss my backpack down and head to the bay with the VW Beetle in it.

Winslow turns the radio up on his side.

Sloane

"Is that your brother?"

"That's Bo."

Not really an answer to my question, but I'm taking it as a *yes.* This Wolf Ridge Body Shop guy is scary as hell. I was given his name as a possible fence for stolen cars, and he panned out. But I don't trust him for a second.

Seeing his younger brother, on the other hand, calms me a bit. He looks as all-American as his older brother looks thug. Yeah, his jeans are ripped and greasy, but a Wolf Ridge High football t-shirt stretches across his bulging muscles, and the rest of him is clean-cut. Good-looking, even.

I'm not used to being treated with the disgust Winslow Fenton has been throwing my way, but I feel better just having his brother here. Like he wouldn't let anything bad happen to me.

And of course, that's probably one of those really stupid assumptions one of those psychology studies would prove shows bias based on good looks. Or clothing. Or general hotness. Just because he's my age and gorgeous doesn't mean he's going to play knight in shining armor if his brother crosses me.

"He's not a part of this," Winslow says, the threat evident in his lowered voice. "Understand?"

"Yeah, definitely. I understand." We're both leaning under the hood of the Porsche, like we're conferring about her horsepower. I have to resist peering into the other bay at Bo's broad back and muscular ass. *Focus, Sloane—jeez.* "So how soon do you think you can get the new title on this?"

"You leave that to me. I'll get it sold. Then I'll give you your cut."

Fuck no.

"That wasn't the deal. You get the title. *I'll* sell it."

He snorts. "You're gonna sell it."

"Yeah, that's what we discussed."

He sneers. "Sorry, honey. No one's gonna buy a six figure Porsche from a sixteen-year-old."

"Seventeen," I correct, although that's not the point.

"If I can steal a car in broad daylight from the Scottsdale Mall, I can pull off the car sale." Turns out, I'm a pretty good hustler. I had to pick up a lot of new skills these last six months.

He gives me a mock apologetic shake of his head. "Sorry, sister. If I get the title, it's mine." He waits a beat. "Right?"

My heart starts pounding harder. This guy is slimy, but I knew that from the beginning. That's the risk associated with stealing cars.

He rubs his nose with a greasy finger, leaving a smear of black on his face. We're nose to nose under the hood. He smells like metal and stale sweat and faintly of the sour alcohol scent people get when they over-indulged the night before.

Now that I've seen his brother, I can see where he might be attractive in a different situation. If he took care of himself and had a decent haircut. And didn't look so damn mean.

I clench my jaw. "We split it fifty-fifty."

"Sixty-forty."

I don't have to guess which one of us gets the sixty.

This guy's going to keep pushing me around. It's going to change to seventy-thirty next time I see him, if I even see him again. I need to get leverage back, and fast.

I draw a deep breath and try to channel my dad. He could talk a guy into anything. And he never used fear to get through to them, the way some salespeople do. Because that's essentially what any con is—a sales job. No, he made them feel good about doing what he wanted. Made them think that's what they wanted too.

"Listen, Winslow." I lean a hip against the bumper of the Porsche. "Like I told you before, I'm looking for a business partner. I already scoped out a Mercedes-Benz S Class at the salvage yard for the next car jack. But if you're the kind of guy who makes a deal and doesn't honor his word, this isn't going to gel going forward. We have to have enough trust between us to make this work."

I throw in words like *honor* and *trust* hoping it might bring out some whisper of those qualities in him, but I doubt he ever had them to begin with.

If I hadn't seen his all-American brother, I wouldn't have even thought of it. But unbelievably, it seems to work.

Winslow draws his chest up and nods. "Fifty-fifty," he concedes. "But I'm selling it."

"We both go," I counter.

He sneers again. "I'm not taking you. You'd fuck it all up. But I'll give you your cut, fair and square."

"You stand to lose more than I do. I'm not eighteen yet. If I get caught, it would be a slap on the wrist. If you get caught, it's a felony."

He pinches his lower lip between his thumb and forefinger, considering me. His gaze darts to his brother, like he's thinking about having Bo sell the car instead. But then he shakes his head. "I'll take the risk."

"I'm coming along," I insist again.

"You're not. Go back to your prep school in Cave Hills and wait until I text you."

My stomach churns. I try not to show my misgivings, though. We're partners, who honor and trust each other. That was the bullshit I was throwing out. I have to walk the talk.

"I need a ride back."

Winslow rolls his eyes and pulls his head out from under the hood of the Porsche. "Fuck." He considers me, then looks over at his brother.

"Bo!"

The younger, far hotter version of him walks over, wiping his hands on a clean white rag. "Yeah?"

"You gotta take this one down to Cave Hills."

He narrows his eyes. "In what?" He throws his arms wide and looks around the place.

"On your bike. Hurry the fuck up. I need you back here to finish that job tonight."

A muscle in Bo's jaw flexes, and he appears to be drawing in a measured breath. "Right. Okay."

He flicks his brows at me and extends his arm like a butler. "This way, *ma'am*."

Okay, maybe he's as big a dick as his brother.

All that hotness wasted on a cocky asshole. Too bad. Not that I was hoping for anything. I just… liked to look.

I follow him to the front of the shop where he picks up a helmet on a motorcycle and hands it to me. "Your limo awaits."

I'm not a total chicken, but I haven't ridden on the back of a motorcycle before. And when I pictured it in the past, it was always riding behind some very trustworthy boyfriend type. Someone hot, but not dick-ish and surly like Bo.

Basically, I'm putting my life in this total stranger's hands.

I take the helmet and swallow.

"Scared, princess?" he sneers. He's wearing a set of dog tags around his neck. Up close, he's even more beautiful than I initially absorbed. He has ice blue eyes that pop against his tanned skin and rumpled brown hair. His lips have a sensuousness to them, but that's the only part. All the rest of him is one hundred percent hard muscle. He probably plays defense, and he probably makes the Cave Hills players cry when he hits them.

I snatch the helmet and toss my hair before I pull it on. It's too big, and I ruin the haughty effect by fumbling with the straps to try to keep the thing on.

To complete the humiliation, Bo steps closer to help me, adjusting the straps until they fit snugly against my chin. His movements are sure and deft, and he completes the action by patting the top of the helmet like I'm a child.

"Aren't you going to wear one?"

"Nah, then I'd have two for the ride home," he says, like that minor inconvenience is much worse than getting his skull smashed in. He produces a pair of sunglasses from the side bag and puts them on. He looks right off the set of a movie. Like a bad boy younger version of Chris Hemsworth. Only way dickier.

I know. That's not a word.

"All set?" He swings a long, thick leg over the seat and looks back. When I gingerly climb on behind him, he gives my wedge sandals a skeptical look. "Normally I wouldn't allow that kind of footwear on the bike, but I guess you don't have much of a choice, do you?"

"Nope."

Uber would've been a good choice.

Why in the hell didn't I Uber this? I was trying to establish this stupid partnership with Winslow. Show some trust to make him trustworthy.

Now look where I am.

About to risk my life on the back of a motorcycle.

He starts the Triumph, and the only warning the asshole gives me that he's going to take off is a look over his shoulder before we lurch.

I bite down a scream and grab his waist in sheer panic. It takes a mile or two before I realize I'm digging my fingers into his skin through the thin t-shirt, but no matter how firmly I tell myself to ease up, I can't.

So much for playing it cool.

Bo stops at a stoplight and turns his head sideways. "You freaking?"

"Nah-o." The one-syllable word becomes two as I lie through my teeth.

He covers one of my clawing hands. His palm is large and rough. Calloused from hard work or maybe playing football—I don't know. He tugs my hand around the front of his body, until it reaches his washboard abs.

"Oh—sorry! Was I hurting you?" I don't normally get flustered by guys. I'm usually the one doing the flustering—especially if we're talking about high school boys. Being five foot nine by seventh grade made it impossible for me to ignore the effect I have on the opposite sex. But I'm a total disaster at this moment.

I blame it all on the motorcycle. It's not from the blue eyes or washboard abs.

His chuckle is low and soft. It shouldn't unexpectedly warm me the way it does. "No chance of that, Legs."

"*Legs?* Is that what you're calling me?"

The light changes, and he takes off again without warning.

I wrap my other arm around his waist, too, so now I'm hugging his back like a freaking koala. Or do they ride on the front? A chimpanzee, then, who has to hold on for dear life while her mama swings from tree to tree.

And then we're zipping onto the highway that leads to Cave Hills. I don't know how many miles it takes for my fear to morph into something different. Something warmer and more alive. By the time we're down the hill, I'm all tingles and awareness, my breath coming in short pants inside the helmet, my hands molded to Bo's abs. The heat from his body radiating into mine. The motorcycle like a giant vibrator between my legs.

I hate that I even find this scenario a turn-on. Motorcycles aren't cool. Boys who ride them are redneck and basic.

Except my body doesn't seem to agree. Or maybe it's not about the motorcycle. Maybe it's about the giant baller whose back I'm glued to.

~

Bo

I PURPOSELY SCARE her because I'm a dick.

I'm a dick, and I *fucking love* making her scream and cling to me for dear life every time I take off too fast.

I also don't mind the way it feels having her snug against my back, her slender arms squeezing in on my ribs every time I lean into a turn.

I'm pretty sure I just heard her mutter, *you suck,* the last time I wove through the lanes of traffic to get ahead.

Serves her right. She's trouble, this one, and she's dragging my brother into it with her.

"Where to?" I ask when we get down to Cave Hills.

"5th and Davidson." She attempts to pry her own hands from me, but I gun the bike, and she seizes me again.

"You're doing that on purpose," she accuses, balling her fists up in the front of my shirt.

She knows what's up. I guess to be a car thief, you'd have to be pretty smart. Or else pretty dumb. But she doesn't strike me as dumb. I saw enough wariness on her face when she was talking to Winslow to know she understands the risks.

I take her to 5th and Davidson. "Now where?"

I half expect her to just get off and not show me where she lives, but she gives me directions to her house. Turns out she doesn't live in one of the many million-dollar homes that make up the wealthy community north of Scottsdale. She's in a townhouse—a nice one—but not that big.

"Right here," she says, pointing. She swings her long leg off the bike and tries to unbuckle the helmet with shaking fingers.

"What's the story with the Porsche?" I ask her point-blank, watching her fumble and not offering my help this time.

I know Winslow isn't going to tell me, and I'm looking for confirmation.

"It's my dad's," she says. "He's out of town, and I put a

dent in it. Your brother said he'd help me fix it without him finding out."

"I didn't see a dent."

"He already fixed it. Now it just needs a little paint." She tears at the straps of the helmet, like I'm holding her hostage with them. "Your brother said he'd get it fixed by tomorrow."

Yeah, right. Total bullshit, of course.

She manages to get it unclasped and yanks the helmet off, tossing out her long thick hair.

I don't want to be stunned by how gorgeous she is up close. I'm looking for some flaw. Some irregularity that can make me dismiss her. But even the large mole on her cheek looks like it was put there just to make her more tempting to guys. Or girls who like girls. Or yeah, pretty much anyone with a pulse.

She doesn't look like she belongs in high school. This girl has probably been frequenting college parties since the day she hit puberty. She's all that.

And I can't fucking stand her for it.

"Thanks for the ride, Bo." She thrusts the helmet at me.

"I didn't catch your name." I ignore the helmet. She seems to be in a huge hurry to get away, and I'm not going to make it easy for her.

"I didn't throw it." She nudges my belly with the helmet, and when I still ignore it, she lets it go and turns on her heel.

I stoop to catch it before it hits the ground. "You don't have to be a cunt," I call out after her. Not because I think she is one—although I'm not ruling it out—I say it more to see if it gets a rise out of her.

It does.

She whirls, her face flushing. "Nice," she nods, walking backward. "Real nice."

I grin because seeing her mad gets my dick hard. "I don't do nice. See you tomorrow, I guess? Will her highness require a pick up?"

I'm watching for a flush or proof of her lie, but she's too good for that. She just flips me the bird as she turns around and unlocks the front door.

Definitely trouble, that one.

And there won't be any talking to Winslow about it. Or stopping him.

I commit her house number to memory. If anything happens to Winslow as a result of this bullshit, I will come down here and rip that entitled Cave Hills bitch apart.

Right after I put her on her knees in front of my open fly.

CHAPTER 2

o

"THE MOON IS ALMOST FULL, GENTS," Coach Jamison preaches in the locker room after practice. We get this lecture every month, and after four years, I can pretty much recite it.

But still—I know it's important shit—especially for the freshmen who are still in the throes of puberty.

"Lock yourselves in your rooms before the game and after the pack run. Do not go anywhere near a female, or" —he holds his hands up— "a male, if that's your interest. I'm not judging."

He paces through the locker room as we filter out of the showers wrapped in towels to stand at our lockers and get dressed. "You boys have raging hormones. You are not safe for the community at large. The moon amplifies your need. It makes you too aggressive. Jack off before the game

—I don't want that much testosterone running through you when we play Lakeside. I can't risk one of you breaking a human's neck.

"And other than jacking your own cocks, you will keep it zippered. I'm not going to warn you to use condoms because *you will not be getting your dicks wet this weekend.*

"Even if you have a girlfriend—*especially* if you have a girlfriend—stay the hell away from her tomorrow night. And I don't subscribe to the *sow your wild oats with humans* philosophy. Boys, you are even less safe to human females right now. They can't defend themselves. If I ever hear one of you forced a girl—human or she-wolf—you are permanently off this team, and I will personally kick your ass. Understood?"

"Yes, Coach Jamison," we all reply.

"Louder."

"*Yes, Coach Jamison,*" we shout, our voices echoing off the metal lockers.

"Wilde, you keep an eye out for every boy on this team during pack run," Coach tells my buddy, who is team captain.

"Yes, sir." He pulls a t-shirt over his head.

Coach lays a lot of pack-alpha responsibility on Wilde, which is one of the reasons I'm glad I wasn't named captain. Yeah, I'm alpha. There's a reason me and my buddies are called the alpha-holes of Wolf Ridge High. But ruling the school and leading a pack are two different things. One comes from a place of rebellion. We flip the bird to everyone but our coach and do whatever the hell we want. We make the social rules at Wolf Ridge High—who is popular. Who gets invited to the mesa. Who's worthy to date.

But Wilde has to uphold rules now. Although Jamison's list of rules is short: No fighting with humans. No impregnating females—human or wolf. No taking a female against her will. No mating bites, even if we think we're in love.

We head out, but our meanest alpha-hole, Cole, hangs back. "Austin, can you take Casey home tonight?"

Abe, Austin's younger brother walks over to catch a ride home, too. He's a sophomore but already playing varsity with us, which says a lot because every guy on this team is an athlete of magnitude.

Austin narrows his eyes at Cole. "Yeah, why?"

We all know why.

Cole showed up to practice with the scent of that human all over him. His next door neighbor—the one he hates because her mom took his dad's job.

Only everyone knows *hate* is pretty fucking close to something else. Something bordering on obsession, if you ask me. I've seen the way he crowds her up against her locker. The way he's always looking for her.

Cole shrugs. "I have to see a teacher about homework."

Uh huh.

But whatever. My dick's hard for a human, too.

I went straight home after dropping the Cave Hills bitch off and yanked it all night. I had her scent all up in my nose. It had rubbed off on the back of my t-shirt where she pressed those luscious breasts against me while we rode, so I took the shirt off and wrapped it around my cock. Pretended she was giving me the handjob to show her gratitude for the ride.

I fell asleep to the image of her tossing that mane of hair over her shoulder with her flippant *I didn't throw it* line as she walked away. Every time I replayed it, I had a different comeback. All of them physical. All of them ending with her on her knees in front of my cock, saying *please may I suck it?*

Yeah, as if *that* ever happens in real life.

The trouble with porn is that it makes regular high school sex about as exciting as sitting through American History class on a half day.

~

Sloane

I UNLOCK my bike after cross country practice and fling my leg over the seat. My legs are still shaking from the long run, but I don't mind the ride home. I think getting in a car and driving would just make my body tighten up. My muscles may be shaky and weak, but pushing them just a little more—in a different way—actually feels good.

Or maybe I'm just a masochist.

My car—or the one my dad let me use—was one of the many assets seized by the government when he went to jail. So maybe I have a little bit of *deserve* wrapped up in riding the bike.

I definitely don't deserve the luxury of a car, and I ought to feel ashamed I ever had one, considering where the money came from. I shake my head to remove the flashes of the days after my dad's arrest. The faces of people who had been my friends, known me my whole life, sneering and turning away from me in scorn as I walked the halls of my old high school to class.

Turns out the sins of the father aren't just visited upon the sons. Daughters inherit that shit too.

I check my phone one more time before I take off to see if there's any message from Winslow.

If I don't get the money by tonight, I'm fucked.

No message.

Dammit.

I lean into the right pedal and take off, riding hard like I can outrun all my father's past transgressions.

I just can't seem to go fast enough today to chase away the shadows around me.

Inside me.

The breeze blows in my face, and I suddenly remember the whip of the wind around me yesterday on the back of Bo's bike. The feel of his hard muscles beneath the slide of his cotton t-shirt. The sound of that deep, growly voice.

My panties get damp, and I rock against the hard lip of the bike seat to alleviate the ache between my legs. I don't know why I find such a cocky asshole so hot, but I do.

It's the bad-boy vibe, I guess. The motorcycle and Rebel Without a Cause attitude.

The ice blue of those eyes judging me for some crime. Whether it's the one I actually committed or a different one, I can't be sure.

All I know is that he doesn't like me.

Neither does his brother, although that bothers me far less.

There's some kind of long-standing rivalry between Cave Hills and Wolf Ridge high. Maybe the animosity stems from that. I don't know—I'm just the new kid here, but I guess Cave Hills' kids are the haves; Wolf Ridge, the have-nots.

I was once one of the haves. I lived in a three-quarter million dollar house in Grosse Pointe, Michigan, the wealthiest suburb of Detroit. My dad was a stock broker.

But if they only knew how far this princess has fallen, they might not hold it against me. The crown has been firmly knocked off my head and crushed underfoot.

My dad went to jail for embezzlement last year, and last month the guards found him hanging in his cell, his bed sheet around his throat. Suicide... allegedly. With everyone my father screwed over, who knows.

I'm living with my mom's sister and my eleven-year-old cousin without a penny to my name. Have been since a little after my father was picked up by the feds.

I TURN onto my aunt's street, and my stomach drops out onto the pavement.

The black Lincoln Navigator that I'm becoming all too familiar with is parked in the lot in front of the townhouses.

The sweat on my skin turns cold and clammy.

I don't make them chase me. I'm not that stupid. I ride my bike right up to the driver's side window.

"Hi guys," I call out brightly, waving my hand beside my face as I peer in.

The window rolls down, and I'm facing two assholes in sunglasses and first class frowns.

They are Vinny and Tom, or as I like to call them, Goon One and Goon Two, even though they look more like middle-aged divorced dads with thinning hair lines and bellies that hang out a little past their belt buckles.

"Where is it?" Vinny demands. He's in a god-awful

peach colored polo, khakis and Ray Bans, like he just came off the golf course.

I pull my phone out of my pocket and check the screen just to see if Winslow messaged yet. Still nothing.

Fucker.

"How'd the greens treat you today, gentlemen? Hit under par?" I try for levity and false confidence.

Tom, in his gray-striped Adidas polo and Titleist hat, opens his mouth like he's about to legit answer, but Vinny's not having it. "Don't be smart, kid." His hand shifts to the console between the seats and rests on a black handgun.

I swallow, my throat suddenly very dry. "I'll have it. There's a lot to go through. But I'm looking. Every day." There's nothing to go through. The few boxes I have of my father's belongings are full of clothes and pictures. My mother's wedding ring…

Tom picks his teeth with a toothpick. "Clock's ticking. Boss'll be back soon."

Sweat trickles down my back. I lean my elbows on the doorframe, enjoying the cool breeze of the A/C, then straighten when both their gazes drift down and lock on my tits. I'm not above using my sexuality whenever necessary, but with these guys, I'm trying to play more of the poor, scared teenage kid role.

I decide to go with the God's honest truth. "Even if I don't find his stuff, I can raise cash to cover it. I stole a Porsche and got a new title for it, but I still have to fence it. When it's sold, I hope to have at least ten grand for you, maybe fifteen. Maybe I could make payments—like until I find it."

I see grudging appreciation on Vinny's face. "That right? You stole a Porsche?"

"Yeah. It'd be easier if you'd take payments in the form of cars. Is that a possibility?"

"No," Vinny says. "We ain't a used car dealership."

"Maybe with a clean title," Tom says at the same time.

But that doesn't work for me. I need Winslow to get the clean title, and that means splitting the profits with him.

I scuff my sneaker in the gravel at my feet. "You sure you can't handle a hot car? I could feed them to you every day, no problem."

Vinny shakes his head. "Nice try, kid. Anyone can steal a car. Moving it is the hard part."

Don't I know it.

"Besides," Tom says. "I doubt boss'd go for it. He's against stealing." Tom's dead serious. I snort a laugh that carjacking is where their boss draws the line. Not kidnapping. Not murder. *Fencing cars.*

They both pull ugly faces at me. I don't like the way Tom's still leering at my breasts. "Boss told you before, he can get a shit ton selling you on the black market. And I just noticed today you have a little cousin."

Ice cold and lava flush through at the same time.

No he fucking didn't.

I sense the blood drain from my face, and they both smile at my terror.

"She looks ripe, that one," Vinny says with a sick smirk. "Perfect age. These pedophiles love the tweens. They go for the most money."

"You stay away from my cousin," I grit through clenched teeth.

"You get the boss his money. *All* his money. He's already pissed it's taking so long."

My stomach is a solid rock of tension. "I'll get it. Stay the hell away from her." I point at them like I'm the mobster doing the shake down. The fact that my finger's shaking probably ruins the whole effect.

It takes me two tries, but I manage to get back on my bike and ride it into the garage of my aunt's townhouse.

I hit the garage door button, and they watch me disappear behind the closed door. I don't cry until I hear the Lincoln drive away and all goes silent. Alone in the dark, the smell of gas and dust filling my nostrils, I gasp for breath between sobs.

Sophie, their golden retriever, woofs and scratches at the door, eager to greet me.

"Just a minute, Soph," I say thickly, wiping my face with both hands.

The door flies open a moment later, and my cousin Rikki regards me as Sophie dashes over to dance around my feet and lick my hands. "Who were those guys?"

Oh shit.

"What guys?" I keep my head ducked, petting the dog as I walk through the door.

"The guys in the black car. They looked like bad news."

"No, they were just asking for directions. But they probably are bad news. Don't stop and talk to strangers like I just did. It's not safe."

"I *know*," she says impatiently. "That's why I was asking."

Inside, the kitchen smells delicious, but I duck past my Aunt Jen quickly. "I'm going to shower," I call out as I dash up the stairs.

"Okay, dinner's almost ready," she calls back.

"Yep. Give me five." I go straight to the en suite bathroom between my room and Nikki's and lock both doors.

Only then do I let myself really cry.

~

Six weeks before

I DON'T KNOW how I'm going to explain the fat lip and bruises to my aunt. I know it's a ridiculous concern considering two men just wrestled me into the back of a black Escalade. They flank me now and a third calmly sits across from us, studying me.

He looks a bit like a cross between Andy Garcia and De Niro. He's in a full tailored black suit, despite the fact that Arizona is literally located on the sun, and it's blistering hot outside. The gaudiest gold and diamond ring I've ever seen is on his left pinky finger.

He raises a salt and pepper brow. "Sloane McCormick?"

"Who's asking?" Adrenaline and fear give my words bite.

His lips twitch, but his eyes remain impassive. Cold. "I'm an associate of your father's."

A stone sinks down, down, down and lodges in my stomach. "I'm not sure if you've heard, but my dad isn't around anymore. He... died recently." My throat works. I haven't seen him in over a year. Haven't been close to him in much longer. I've cried all the tears that could be cried, but saying it out loud somehow makes it fresh.

"His passing is why I'm here." He snaps his fingers and flicks his hand this way and that, and the two goons holding me in place let me go. He leans in, elbows on knees, hands folded in prayer. "Your father had something of mine—my cut, if you will—and he hid it for safekeeping. His cellmate told my guy you know where it is."

I shake my head, confused. "All his assets were frozen—"

"This wasn't something the Feds knew about. Think real hard, *bella mia*. Did he send you any letters, maybe something in code, maybe had a location on it? A number sequence?"

Ice trickles down my spine. My father sent me letters. Letters I never opened. Letters I crumpled up and sent out in the trash because I was pissed that he ruined my life.

I shake my head again, this time not looking at him.

"That's too bad." He sits back and cocks his head. "Such a pretty girl, you are. It will be such a travesty when you go missing." He flicks his wrists again and a black cloth sack covers my head.

Panic surges through my veins, my vision going spotty. "Wait! Wait!" I fight the men at my sides. "I have his papers. From his office. Boxes that are in storage." The sack is whipped off, and I suck in air like I'd been strangled. "Just tell me what you're looking for. I'll find it."

He gives me a soft smile as if I've performed as he hoped I would. "There are six gold bars the size of your iPhone and a little oil painting of birds. It's a rare piece done by Camille Pissarro early in his career. It's all worth more than your life, but if you can't find it, I'll be happy to see what I can get for you on the black market. I know a few buyers who would love a pretty toy like you."

Gold bars? A painting? Like a treasure hunt? My mind spins and pings like a pin ball bouncing back and forth, up and down. Finally, it hits and sinks in at *I know a few buyers who would love a pretty toy like you.*

"It's just your luck I have to go out of the country on unexpected business. You have a few months before I'm back in the states. More than enough time, no? And while I'm gone, Tom and Vinny here will stay back and keep an eye on you. I wouldn't want you to think of running off or contacting any agents of the law before we can reunite."

Without another word, I'm shoved out of the SUV and land on hands and knees, the asphalt ripping open skin. I barely feel it. I'm numb. Shaking.

"And *bella mia,*" he calls out the open door. "I almost forgot. My condolences on your father's *untimely* death."

CHAPTER 3

o

I'M the only one in the shop Saturday morning because Uncle Greg decided he's taking weekends off now, and Winslow is still sleeping off last night.

I'm guessing he sold the stolen Porsche because he was waving cash around yesterday, making a big deal out of buying the weekly groceries for our mom and asking what bills she needed paying off. I heard him making plans with his friend, Ben, to hit the Phoenix nightclubs last night, and he stumbled in at dawn this morning reeking of alcohol.

Cole's not in yet, I'm guessing he's jerking off while looking in his next door neighbor's window to keep himself from busting down her door.

Fates know, *I'm* feeling the full moon.

I couldn't sleep at all last night, and my balls were blue over another certain human.

Wilde and Austin lounge against a Buick all sweaty from their morning run. They're the most motivated of the mini-pack I call friends—the alpha-holes. They get up and run every morning because Coach drilled the habit into us as underclassmen when we needed to keep our raging hormones from erupting into inappropriate aggression—sexual or otherwise. It works. I would totally do it, but I don't have time with my duties at the shop.

As if conjured by the moon herself, a tow truck pulls up with a smashed up Mercedes behind it. And guess who's sitting in the passenger side of the truck?

Uh huh.

Miss no-name human female who has me fucking my hand all night while I curse her gorgeous face.

"Get lost, you guys," I growl at my friends, which of course, only makes them crane their necks to see what I'm seeing.

"Is she the Cave Hills car thief?" Wilde asks.

Stupid me, I made the mistake of mentioning her as HILF—human I'd like to fuck—when Cole was grousing about his human neighbor.

"I said, *get lost.*"

Those sexy long legs emerge from the passenger side door.

"Now, or I'll fucking kill you both."

Austin chuckles. He's the most good-natured of all of us. There's a reason he's class president and a first-class player. "Find out if she has any friends—leaving!" he laughs when I growl, and the two of them pick up their water bottles and take off.

I pick up a clean rag and stride over, wiping my hands.

"Where do you want it?" the tow truck guy calls out. I know her game. She's bringing in the totalled Mercedes to use for the salvage title. Then she steals a matching car, Winslow swaps a few identifying parts, and *voila*—she has a clean title to sell the jacked car.

I cock my head and catch the eyes of Legs. "We don't."

Her steps falter, the swing of her hips hitches. "Winslow already knows about this." She waves in my direction. "Is he here?"

I saunter closer. "Nope."

I see her gaze skitter over my shoulders and across my chest before snapping back to my face. "Well, he's going to be working on it. So where would *he* want it?"

I fold my arms across my chest, ignoring the tow truck driver's impatient throat clearing. I give her a solid stare-down, pulling the alpha-wolf method of waiting until she blinks away before I jerk my thumb. "Around back."

I'm pretty sure we don't want all these luxury cars sitting out where people can see them. Especially not if this is going to become a regular thing.

Fuck.

What is Winslow into now? This could sink us all.

I don't move as the driver pulls the truck around back and unloads the car.

I don't move when Legs pays the guy cash from a wad she pulls from her back pocket.

I still don't move when she makes her way back to me.

"Sloane," she says.

It takes me a beat to understand she's answering my question from days before.

Right. Because now she wants something from me.

Only because the moon is full tonight, she might get it.

I stick out my hand. "Bo."

Her handshake is firm, and the moment my skin touches hers, I feel a little drop in my stomach—like when an elevator comes to a stop.

"Are you the only one around today?"

My dick punches against my zipper, even though I doubt she's suggesting anything. Still, her sultry voice and those long, long legs have me at a disadvantage.

Damn moon.

I play it cool, though. "Mmm hmm. Why?"

She glances around. I know she's about to ask for a favor, I'm just not sure what flavor it will be. When she does, it surprises me.

"Can you teach me?"

"Excuse me?"

"I don't know. The basics. How to change out an engine, or something."

I snort and take a step forward into her space. I pick up a lock of her thick copper hair and twirl it around my finger.

I'm surprised when she doesn't immediately toss her head to free it, but then, she wants something.

"I get it, Legs. You want to cut Winslow out of the situation. Learn to do this on your own."

Actually, that's not a bad idea.

This girl has the potential to ruin our lives, but as the younger brother, I'm not strong enough yet to challenge Winslow on his shit. And I'm not low enough to rat him out to pack elders.

She rubs her lips together. They are full and soft—definitely kissable.

Except I'm not imagining kissing them. I'm imagining devouring them. Biting, sucking, twisting my mouth over hers until she gasps for breath.

"There's no situation," she maintains.

Okay, so that's how we're playing this.

"Did Winslow make some dire threat if you bring me into this?" Of course he did. My brother may go off half-cocked most of the time, but there's one thing our mom drilled into him—keep me out of it.

She needs one Golden Boy.

There's a flicker behind her eyes. A hesitation. I'm guessing she's not sure how to play me. Let me in to build trust or keep pretending, even though we both know it's a lie.

I wait because I'm curious. Fuck that, I'm downright fascinated with this chick. None of her makes sense. She's a total enigma. Rich hottie from Cave Hills is stealing cars and putting the hustle on people? It shows intelligence and ingenuity.

But I also scent a whiff of desperation in her.

This isn't a bored, white rich girl entertaining herself with jacking cars.

There's need wrapped in there. Some kind of trouble at the base of it.

But what could it possibly be?

She goes for acknowledging the lies with tone of voice. "Again, don't know what you're talking about." She catches my hand at her hair to stop the twirling, and once more, I experience the elevator drop.

Fucking full moon.

Wolves aren't supposed to get this horned up over humans.

"I'll pay you."

I don't know why that makes my dick hard. I think it's the husky way she says it, like she's some rich socialite offering her pool boy money to put suntan lotion on her back. Or whatever the cliche is.

I can't stop the upward twist of my lips. "Yeah? How much?"

I watch the calculation in her eyes and expect a low-ball. "Hundred an hour."

I bite back the splutter of surprise. Well, I guess it makes sense—she just got the proceeds from the Porsche. She's reinvesting her income.

"Winslow shows up, he'll kick your ass."

Now I see a flicker of a smile on her lips. She knows I'm going to say yes. "I'll take my chances."

I shrug. "Brave for such a small thing."

She snorts. "Only you could call me small, Muscles."

I smile down at her. She looks up at me. We're having a moment—which is not what I wanted here. This girl is total trouble, but I'm drawn like a magnet to metal.

"I'm probably gonna get my ass kicked for this," I say because if Winslow catches me, it's me he's going to whup.

"Come on." I lead her to the garage to grab a few tools and hand her a socket wrench. "You're going to do the work. I'll supervise."

A soft gust of air comes out of her. Almost a chuckle. "I'll bet you'll like that, too."

"Telling you what to do? You know it." I lead her around back. I can't pop the hood on the Mercedes because it's crushed closed, so I use the jaws of life and pry the fucker off. We're not repairing this car, so it doesn't matter, anyway.

"All right, dropping the engine." I beckon her over to me. "First thing we do is disconnect the battery and drain the fluids."

I walk her through it, and all the while, her scent fills my nostrils, reminding me of how it felt to have her riding on the back of my Triumph, those thighs parted behind me, those arms wrapped tightly around my waist.

I want to get those legs apart in a different way this time.

But I detect the slightly acrid smell of fear, so I give her space. She's nervous.

I like her nervous, and I like ordering her around, but there's a subtle line here I don't wanna cross. On edge is one thing—actually scared is another.

She doesn't know what she's doing, and some of the clamp bolts on the hoses are too hard for her to unscrew. I watch her struggle with one for a while before she straightens and looks over her shoulder. "Little help?"

I grin and slide off the hood of the old Mustang I've been working on refinishing. "I was wondering if you'd ask."

She makes a scoffing sound. "You could've offered."

"I was timing how long you'd struggle on your own. Three minutes and forty-eight seconds. Controlling much?"

I step in close to smother her effect of shocked outrage. She's trying to hand me the wrench, but I don't take it. Instead, I cover her hand and position myself behind her. "Your angle was wrong, that's all." I cage her between my two arms and lean forward forcing her to practically fold herself over the car. I want to grind my erection into her heart-shaped ass, but I resist. If I go there, I might not be able to pull back. Plus, that would actually constitute harassment. Which I'm not totally above, depending on the circumstances.

Again, subtle line.

I guide her hand to secure the bolt in the socket wrench. Truth is— it wasn't the angle. She's just not strong enough, but I wanted to get my arms around her. Breathe her scent up close. Keep her on edge and a little turned on.

It's working because I detect the scent of her arousal like a heady perfume.

It makes my head swirl.

With a cock of my wrist, I pry the bolt loose and step back.

Breathe the scents of the shop and autumn air, already turning hot as the morning's gone on.

Try to get my head back.

"Thanks," she says softly, without turning around.

Damn Cave Hills princess and her perfect ass luring me into making a colossal full moon mistake.

SLOANE

MY SKIN PRICKLES EVERYWHERE. I still feel his heat at my back, even though he stepped away. I don't know what to think about this guy. He's a cocky dick, for sure.

But so. Hot.

Last time we were together, I would've sworn he hated me—he blew so much scorn and derision my way. And that's still present today. But he's also coming on to me.

Touching my hair.

Molding his body against mine to loosen the bolt, those military dog tags he wears clinking softly between us.

The big brawny jerk makes my knees go weak.

And I'm not usually what they call boy-crazy. In fact, when I moved to Cave Hills to live with my aunt and cousin, I told everyone I had a serious boyfriend back home just to keep myself out of the dating pool. After the mafia guy's men showed up, it became even more important that I not get too close to anyone. Those maniacs will go after anyone.

I don't have time for boys. Not when I have to steal a car every few weeks to feed the mafia monster.

Besides, me getting close to someone would only make them a target, as I learned last week with the asshole's threat against my cousin.

I stop and wipe my forehead. The air's getting hot—October in Arizona still feels like a summer day back in Michigan. Or maybe I'm just hot from having Muscles spooning me from behind.

"Harder than you imagined?" It's not quite a jeer, so I answer honestly.

"Yeah. I don't know if I could do it on my own. Not if the bolts are that tight."

He tips his head. "I'm sure you could pay a guy a hundred bucks an hour to loosen bolts."

"Are you offering?"

"Nope. I'm staying the hell away from all the trouble you bring. That's the only reason I'm teaching you right now, Legs. I want your operation out of this shop."

That shouldn't hurt my feelings. It's exactly what I

want, too. And yet the familiar sensation of being unwanted hits me squarely in the chest.

I've always been trying to prove I'm worth keeping. My mom died in childbirth, and even though my dad never came out and said it, I know he blamed me. So I worked hard to make him happy. To not be any trouble. To make him believe her death wasn't for nothing.

But it never worked.

And now he's dead, too, and I'm trying to be invisible in my aunt's house. Trying to make up for his crimes with crimes of my own.

He cocks his head, studying me, and I get the irritating notion he read my hurt, even though I have a stellar poker face.

Of course, that pisses me off. I flip the socket wrench in the air and catch it. "Why don't you show off a little, Muscles, and loosen the rest of them?"

He wanted me to ask for help? I'll ask.

The sooner I get this over with and get away from his scrutiny, the better. I am very much doubting my ability to do this on my own—I should just throw in the towel now.

He smirks and takes the wrench. In about five seconds, he loosens every bolt and sets the socket wrench down. Then he removes the hoses and drains the fluids into a pan he shoves below.

"Hey princess, go empty this in the barrel inside." He thrusts the pan of fluids at me.

I try not to show my distaste at touching the grimy pan and my fear of it sloshing all over me.

Maybe I really am a princess.

I gingerly take the dripping pan and hold it out in front of me to go in.

When I get back, the car is up on jack stands.

Which doesn't make sense.

I didn't hear him start the engine—hell, I already know the thing doesn't drive, or I wouldn't have had to tow it here.

"How'd you get the car up there?"

"I pushed it."

Dayum. That definitely gets me hot and bothered. This guy may still be in high school, but he's about as manly as they get. I mean, he's over six feet of solid muscle, he knows his way around a car and back, and apparently can single-handedly push them around his garage with total ease.

My body tingles with some primitive reaction to his physical prowess. Like the cave girl in me just realized he would be the very best choice for a mate. Not only would we make beautiful babies—not that a cave girl thinks about that—but he'd be able to beat off our predators with a club and make sure we survived through the winter.

"Did that excite you?"

I scoff, but search his face. Again, I didn't think I was showing anything in my expression.

Turns out, it wasn't my expression that gave me away.

Bo is staring at the twin points of my nipples, jutting through my sports bra and t-shirt.

I fold my arms across my chest. "As if. Listen, I think you're right. This is more than I can handle. How about I just pay you for the hour and get out of your hair?"

He saunters over to me. He has this casual way of moving. It's strange to watch a guy so big move with so much grace and ease. "Okay." If I didn't know better, I would say he sounds disappointed. "I'll take your money. How are you getting home?"

I fully planned on calling an Uber. I really did.

I don't even know what comes over me when I tip my face up and turn my flirt on. "Feel like a drive to Cave Hills?"

He plucks the one hundred dollar bill out of my fingers, and I get the feeling it's a lot of money for him.

Not that it's not to me, but I've been dealing in huge deficits and big payments. I'm getting used to handling large amounts of cash.

Spoken like a true criminal.

"It'll cost you," he tells me. I think he's going to ask for more money, but he surprises me by getting real. "Take your next car somewhere else, Legs. We can't handle this kind of heat here. My brother acts tough, but he's in over his head, and I'm guessing you are, too. So after this one, retire. Or find a new mechanic. Just don't come back. Understand?"

For some reason, I can't breathe with him standing so close. He's not threatening me, but I almost prefer his snarl over this honest appeal. And again, I experience a sense of rejection, which is totally stupid.

"Sounds like Uber would be cheaper."

He drops his head to the side. "Yeah, I thought you'd say that. Get on the bike, Legs."

I don't know why the stupid nickname is starting to grow on me. It's totally derogatory to refer to a female by one of her body parts. And yet my chest gets warm when he says it, like I'm celebrating the fact that he's given me a pet name.

Utterly ridiculous.

I'm also celebrating him taking me home. Which is even more ridiculous. Being attracted to a guy who thinks so little of me is a problem. A total mistake.

So getting excited about nesting behind him on his bad ass bike is an even bigger mistake, but here I am, doing exactly what he said. Getting on his bike and putting on the helmet as I watch him lock up the shop.

And I shouldn't get so fluttery imagining I'm so special because he closed Wolf Ridge Body Shop during store hours to drive me home, but I do.

I get off the bike to give him room to get on and then throw my leg over the seat to sit behind him. He has the nerve to thump my thigh like I'm his horse before he kicks the motorcycle to life and lurches out of the parking lot.

I catch my breath and cling to him, my body a live wire of tension and excitement.

Like this drive is going to end in something far more than me getting off and walking in my house.

Like this drive means anything at all.

Like meeting Bo Fenton isn't the only bright spot under this cloud of darkness that's engulfed me ever since my dad went to jail.

Christ, I need to get my head on straight. I have to raise six gold bars worth of money, whatever that is, or my cousin and I will both be sold to sick perverts with bankrolls who make real life torture porn as a hobby. This is no time to fall for the cocky jerk who treats me like dogshit and drives a bike like a dream.

CHAPTER 4

Three weeks later

Bo

On the day everything goes to shit, you don't wake up thinking, *Today my whole life changes...*

Sheriff Gleason's tires screech as he whips into the school parking lot, gets out, and jogs to meet Coach at the side of the field.

"Fenton!" Coach laces every bit of wolf authority in his voice when he yells my name during practice. He's standing with the sheriff on the side of the field, and a wave of foreboding flashes through me.

I pull off my helmet and stalk over.

"Get in the car," the sheriff demands.

"Why?"

Coach is beside me, his big palm on my nape a warning. "It's Winslow."

"Fuck."

You know how they say time stands still in moments of crisis?

Well it was like that, except the opposite. Time speeds up. Or just disappears—I don't know. The world seems to whirl around me, but I can't make sense of any of it.

Sheriff Gleason is here. Coach's hold on me is crushing and should be an anchor, but it's propelling me to the back of a cop car. I don't want to get in. I know Winslow is in trouble, but why am I getting hauled in? But I don't ask any of the million questions blazing through my mind. I climb in the back of the squad car. The door slams. Sheriff Gleason drives me to his office where my mom and Uncle Greg sit waiting, looking like someone died.

"What is it?" I demand. "What happened?"

"Your brother got caught by human police selling a stolen vehicle today, son," Sheriff Gleason says. "He resisted arrest."

"And they shot him!" my mother bellows, tears streaming down her face.

My gaze snaps to the sheriff for verification, and he nods. "They thought he was drawing a weapon. He was shot but still escaped. Which means he's probably fine."

"How do we know? What if he was shot in the head?" my mother cries.

"Then they would've found a body," Sheriff Gleason reasons. And while his logic is sound, mentioning *body* to my mother was a mistake because she breaks down in sobs again.

Winslow's a shifter, like everyone in this room, which means chances are extremely high he's fine. He probably shifted to push the bullet out and to speed his healing and ran for the mountains. My mom knows that, but she still has PTSD from my dad's death, and shit like this upsets her.

I walk over to her, and she stands up and throws herself at me.

I wrap her up in my arms and squeeze. She's a foot shorter than I am and thin from hard work and the pain of living after losing her mate.

I kiss the top of her head. "It will be all right, Mom. Winslow's fine."

My mom pushes me away. "Do you know something?" She uses her most fierce mama wolf voice, and I take a step back.

I don't want to lie.

I definitely don't want to lie.

But like I said before, I won't throw Winslow under a bus with pack elders, which means my mom and great uncle and the sheriff.

And the damn alpha.

I almost groan when Alpha Green strides in, eyes narrowed, his aging body radiating power. I stifle the involuntary shiver that runs through my body to be in his presence.

"Alpha Green," I mutter, keeping my eyes down and my throat exposed.

"Everyone into my office," Sheriff Gleason commands.

My mom shoots me a look of pure betrayal as we all shuffle in, and my stomach drops to my shoes.

Sheriff Gleason's office feels too small for all of us—mainly because Alpha Green's sheer force of will fills the place. Plus, he and the sheriff are big guys, and I'm almost full grown myself.

Uncle Greg looks old—so old—as he scrubs a hand across his greying stubble.

My mom appears destroyed, and that's the part that fucking kills me. It makes me want to tear this room apart. As if that would help.

A silence descends and everyone focuses on the alpha. Who focuses on me.

I swallow.

"What do you know about this, Bo?"

Fuck. He has an incredible ability to instill fear. It's some primitive pack biology. He looks, I quiver.

I may think I'm a big man. I may scare the shit out of the little football players from other teams. But in here, I'm just a kid. I have no power and barely a will of my own.

I try to stick to the truth. With a slow, sorry shake of my head, I say, "I wasn't part of it."

"You better not have been a part of it!" my mother splutters as my uncle growls, "Damn straight."

"That wasn't the question, son," the sheriff has to point out.

Damn the shaking. There's no hiding it—every wolf in here will smell my fear.

"I suspected it," I say. Again, not a lie. No one confirmed or denied the operation to me. I look over at my uncle. "The Porsche. And the Mercedes."

"Yeah," Uncle Greg says dryly. "I figured that much out."

"Is he stealing the cars?" the sheriff demands.

I draw in a breath, then shrug. "I don't think so," I mumble. Covering for Winslow has been part of my M.O. since I was a tot. I don't know why I'm dead set on not revealing Sloane's involvement, though.

"So who is?" Alpha Green wants to know.

This is the fucking hard part. The impossible part. My will against alpha will.

I drop my eyes and scuff my huge red Nike hightops on the floor. "I don't know," I lie.

I lift my eyes and take in four dubious faces. I'm sure they think it was Ben Thomasson, my brother's no-good friend who he's been helling around with since the beginning of time. Or some human gang situation.

"Tell me everything you know about this, right now," Alpha Green demands with alpha power. Aggression plows me in the center of the chest. No one moves, yet I feel it hit me in the sternum and push me back in my seat. It's not just from the alpha—it's from every male wolf in the room.

Only my mom looks at me with trust shining in her eyes.

She's always believed in me. Always hung her hopes on my success. That's why she wants me to go to college. Get ahead in the pack.

I clear my rusty voice. "I don't know anything, sir. Like I said, I suspected, but Winslow purposely kept me out of it. He told me to mind my own business when I brought it up."

Alpha Green stares a hole into me so large a fist would fit through it. He knows I'm holding something back, and he's pissed as hell.

"Well, if you get in touch with Winslow, give him my message—he needs to come before council in the next twenty-four hours, or he's banished."

My mom chokes back a sob.

And he's banished is probably more like it. I'm sure

council's edict would be for him to turn himself in or be banished, anyway.

"I'll tell him, sir. If I hear from him."

Alpha Green's still giving me the death glare. "Bo, if I *ever* hear you were a part of this operation or if you become a part of this operation, son..."

"I'm not. You won't. I swear to fate," I interrupt.

He lifts his chin. "Go."

I stand up. No one else moves, so I guess I'm the only one dismissed. Or the adults are going to discuss me when I leave. Fuck.

I walk out. My bike's still at school, so I text Wilde for a pick up. He and the other alpha-holes are blowing up my phone to find out what happened.

While I stand there, my mind whirls around what to do.

And every thought is centered around Sloane. That Cave Hills bitch who brought all this shit down. I'm going down there, *right fucking now*, to have a word with her.

A few words.

Austin, Wilde and Slade pull up in Wilde's Jeep and yank me in on a rolling stop.

Cole isn't with them—probably because he's only about Bailey now and has been since the full moon run, when my asshole brother and his friends cornered and attacked her, and we had to fight them off—*in wolf form.*

Which means she knows what we are.

I honestly don't know how Cole's gonna handle that shit with the alpha, but so far, none of us have breathed a word. Not Winslow and his buddies—because they were at fault. And definitely not us.

I've literally been best friends with these guys since I

was born. They are more like brothers to me in terms of having my back than Winslow will ever be. In fact, most of the time, it's been us against Winslow and his buddies, who were always hell on wheels.

"What happened?" Wilde demands immediately.

"Fucking Winslow. Got shot by human cops trying to sell a stolen car. I guess they thought he was drawing a weapon."

Austin whistles. "Where is he?"

"Don't know. He ran. We're assuming he's fine. If he were shot in the head, the cops would've found him." Unless a bullet is made of silver, it won't stop a wolf. Not unless it blows his brains out. Not even a wolf can recover from that shit.

I realize Wilde is driving toward my house. "Hang on. Take me back to school. I need to get my backpack and bike."

"You sure? I can drive you to school tomorrow."

"I'm sure. I need my bike now. I have something to do. And you guys? I may not be in school tomorrow, but cover for me, and tell Coach I'll make it to the game, if he'll let me play."

I have a half-baked plan of how to fix this shit. And it involves getting so far up in Sloane's business she'll rue the day she stepped in Wolf Ridge.

"He'll let you play," Wilde promises, even though it would be a violation of district rules. You have to be in school that day if you want to participate in any sporting event.

Wilde whips into the school parking lot and parks by my bike.

"Thanks," I call, already halfway out.

"You going after the girl?" Wilde calls out. Because true friends know what you're going to do before you even do.

"Yep."

"Give her hell!" Austin yells with a grin.

"Oh, I will."

I'm coming for you, Legs.

And there will be hell to pay.

SLOANE

I WIN first place at the Cave Hills Cross Country Invitational and jog it off to cool down before I go back to cheer on my teammates. It's past dinnertime, and my stomach's starting to complain as the sunset paints the craggy rocks of Wolf Ridge pink and purple.

This is my favorite time of day in Arizona. There's nothing like the way the mountain glows.

The peace isn't real, though. I always have that sense of stealing the moment. Like I don't deserve to enjoy sunsets or mountains or anything about my life in Arizona.

The meet finally ends, and we filter down to the locker rooms, everyone dragging ass now. I see the large figure leaning up against the building, but he doesn't set off any flares of warning. He's not one of the guidos sent to rough me up—I'm expecting them in a couple more days. He looks like a football player.

It's not until he starts moving toward me that I realize exactly *which* football player. Not one from my school.

Bo. And he's coming at me like he's mad.

I veer to head him off. The last thing I need is him saying something in front of my teammates.

He stalks up to me—I mean *right* up to me. Like, in my space, his huge muscled chest almost bumping me before he stops. "*What. Happened?*" His voice is low and mean. It's an accusation.

A chill washes over me. "I don't know." I search his face. "You tell me."

Tension radiates from his shoulders, a muscle flexes in his jaw. "The cops shot my brother, that's what happened. When he was trying to sell the car. I'm guessing you weren't there?"

More ice rushes through me. "Is he—is he all right? Did he live?"

Bo shrugs. "He's gone. He got away. You haven't heard from him?"

I shake my head. "Why would I?"

"You're partners, right? You stole the car—he got the title?"

It's stupid at this point not to confirm what he obviously already knows, but I maintain a blank face.

He curses and looks away, hands balled into fists. I take a step back. I don't think he's dangerous, but the guy is huge, and his anger makes him intimidating.

When his gaze returns, his eyes look more silver than blue—an odd trick of the light. "I'm on you like glue, Legs. Wherever you go, I go. Until Winslow shows up. Understand?"

I throw my hands in the air. "I'm not hiding your brother, Bo. He's not going to come to me. I don't have any money—*he* was supposed to get it. So now we're both fucked."

Bo's scrutiny sharpens. "Why are you fucked, Legs?" His voice is soft and dangerous.

A hot prickle runs up my neck. For one millisecond, I want to tell him. Everything. I want to tell one other human being, so I'm not alone in this thing.

But I have to stay alone, or I sink his ship, too.

He reaches out and cages my arm, his grip coaxing rather than steely.

I affect a loose shrug. "No car. No money." I turn to leave before he can pry more, but he holds on to my arm and rubberbands me back to face him, causing me to bounce off his very solid chest. The dog tags he wears jingle with the impact. He wraps his other arm around my back to steady me, and we're both caught for a second—staring into each other's eyes. His glint silver again. They're beautiful. He's really a spectacular specimen of manhood.

Samantha and Teri, my friends from the team, choose this compromised moment to walk up.

"You didn't tell me Tyler was visiting," Samantha gushes.

I shove away from Bo harder than necessary because he chooses that moment to let go. Once more, I'm off-balance. Lightning fast, his hand shoots out to catch my elbow and steady me.

"Oh, ah—" I stutter.

"This is Tyler?" Teri asks with delight, sticking her hand out for him to shake. Both my teammates ogle Bo, which is understandable, but they have it all wrong. "It's so nice to finally meet the long-distance boyfriend! We've heard all about you. You flew out to take her to Homecoming?"

I'm usually quick with lies or coverups, but for some reason, this whole scene throws me off my game. Their assumption that Bo is the boyfriend I made up to keep things simple makes my cheeks get hot and prickly.

I wait for his firm rejection, but before I even know what's happening, Bo bands an arm around my waist from behind and pulls me sharply back against his hard body. There's aggression in the movement. Like he's pissed about something. That I have a boyfriend?

"Of course, I flew out for Homecoming," he purrs in my ear, the mocking in his voice making me blush hotter. "I wouldn't miss it for the world."

"Aw, that's so sweet," Teri says, eyeing Bo appreciatively. "You two are going to look great."

Samantha looks at me. "Was it a surprise visit? I thought you said you couldn't go."

Bo strokes my side and nuzzles at my neck. "Yep. I surprised her. And I can't wait to take her to the dance." His lips brush my ear.

I hate him. I had one second there to declare he's not Tyler, and I missed it. Maybe I was distracted by how strong his arm felt around me. Or his clean, masculine scent. Or pretending, just for a moment, that he was my imaginary boyfriend.

But now I'm screwed.

Because his hands are all over me, and he's purposely torturing me. There's an element of mockery that runs through every word he says. Like the idea of being my boyfriend is so stupid and ridiculous and he's milking the moment for as long as possible.

Until he delivers some evil punchline.

Or shoves me away.

Or gets me all hot and bothered and laughs about his power over me.

Because the power is affecting my body like a potent drug. Heat tingles everywhere he touches. My pussy clenches. I elbow him in the ribs to free myself, but he tickles me like this is one of our games.

"Stop it," I squirm away from him, pissed he's making me smile against my will. Tickling should be outlawed in every country.

"Hey, it was nice to meet you two," Bo says, lacing his fingers firmly through mine and tugging me toward the parking lot.

I stop and try to pull my hand away. "My stuff's still inside," I say.

"Oh, okay." He frees me but crosses his arms over his massive chest. "I'll wait."

"No, really." I fake a smile. "Go on home. I have my bike here, and I have to ride it."

"Okay," he says in a *if-you-say-so* tone. "I'll see you at home, then." He pumps his eyebrows. It's damn sexy, even though it makes me want to throat punch him.

My fake smile gets more brittle. "Bye, then."

He lifts his fingers and waves like a little girl. "Bye, sugarpie."

I roll my eyes as I turn away. "He's being an idiot," I tell Samantha and Teri. "He doesn't call me sugarpie."

He doesn't call me anything.

Unless *Legs* or *princess* counts, but they are far less terms of endearment than monikers to demean me.

Sugarpie.

What an asshole. I seriously could slap him silly.

~

Bo

I DON'T KNOW who the fuck Tyler is, but the alpha in me wants to rip him apart. After I outperform him in every arena possible.

As if humans could even compete with our shifter games. It would be dating games, then. The need to prove he's inferior to me in every way courses through my body as I stride to the Triumph and swing my leg over the seat.

Fucking human boyfriend.

I'll bet he's a shitty kisser.

Twenty bucks she's never even come with him. I don't know what the stats are, but I think it's hard to make a human girl orgasm during sex. I forget where I heard that —Coach, maybe. I think he was telling us with the advice to spend time trying to solve that puzzle. Make sure she gets off every time you do.

I kick my motorcycle to life and ride in the direction of Sloane's house, stopping at In-N-Out Burger to wolf down three burgers and two orders of french fries. When I get to her townhouse, I park the bike up the street a ways and walk back, sticking to the shadows. Night has fallen, and the full moon of last weekend is waning. At least I'm not fighting that edge with the human.

No, I'm just here to make her suffer for what happened with Winslow. It should've been her who got caught. Sloane's the damn car thief. This was her stupid operation. If she never would've shown her beautiful face up in Wolf Ridge, I'd still have a big brother around to be man of the house. Take care of my mom and run the shop for our great uncle.

Now it all fucking falls on me.

My mom's dream of me getting a college scholarship and leaving Wolf Ridge died today.

Thanks to Sloane.

I text my mom, *Spending the night at Austin's. We have a big project due and have to work late.* My mom won't like it, not with grieving the Winslow situation, but Austin's the good kid in the group. His dad is a doctor and a pack elder. My mom won't worry about me if she thinks I'm with him.

I text Austin, too, so he can cover for me, if he needs to.

I swear, sometimes I think my life just ended up fifty times better than Winslow's because of the friends I fell in with. I got lucky—both Austin and Wilde are pack royalty. Cole used to be before his mom left with our math teacher and his dad started drinking. Slade and I somehow landed with the golden boys, which means we make the right decisions—we protect the females, mentor the younger wolves. We might be dicks, but we're still the good kids.

Winslow and his pack of friends? They were always causing trouble. They're the ones we protect the females from. The ones getting into drunk driving wrecks or knocking up humans while still in high school.

Winslow didn't have great role models. Plus, he was older when our dad died—it made him act out as a teen. I don't know how he's going to get out of the shitpile he's got himself into this time, but I feel obligated to help. Even if he doesn't ask for it.

I circle the townhouse, observing.

Sloane's home—her scent is fresh near the garage.

Lights are on in the bedrooms upstairs. One of the bedrooms is right over the porch roof, making it easily accessible to anyone who knows how to climb.

Like me.

Not that climbing is my regular gig, but anything physical is a done deal with me. I'm a shifter athlete in my prime. I jump, catching the overhang with my fingertips and swinging one leg up, then the other. The biggest problem is keeping quiet as I pad toward the window. To my right, I can see through the curtains of the other window, not accessible from the roof.

A small figure sits on the bed—a tween girl. Not Sloane.

Her little sister, maybe?

I inch toward the other window and peek through the crack in the curtain.

Bingo.

Sloane's moving around the room—oh, fuck. I lose my breath. She's peeling off her clothes.

If I were more of a dick, I'd stay and watch the show. She has magnificent tits under that running bra, I just know it. But she's about to pull off her shorts, and I don't feel right about perving anymore.

I tap the window lightly.

A dog barks from the other bedroom, full five-alarm barking. She barrels into the room through what appears to be a bathroom—it must connect the two bedrooms—and runs right for the window.

Smart dog.

Beautiful, too. A golden retriever.

I let the wolf in me come to the surface and send a push of dominance through the window. It's not something you learn. It's something you either have or don't. What makes one wolf more alpha than the other. It's an energy that comes out when you need to establish it's your will over another's.

The dog instantly stops barking and whines.

Sloane yanks the curtain back, eyes flared wide. To her credit, she doesn't scream.

I hold a finger to my lips and point at the window. "Let me in," I mouth.

She shakes her head.

I frown, exaggerating a look of disapproval in my expression. "Now, Legs."

The dog whines again. I must've sent another push of dominance.

Apparently, it works on humans, too, because Sloane flips the lock on the window and drags it to the side. "What are you doing here?" she whisper-shouts.

I step through the window, ducking so I don't hit my head. "I told you, princess. White on rice."

"You told me glue, but whatever. You can't be here. And what did you do to Sophie?"

The dog is in full submission, tail tucked, head down, nose on the floor.

"Good girl, Soph," I say, and she springs back up, tail wagging. I reward her by stroking her face and ears and thumping her body. She's a sweet pet.

Wolves generally don't keep dogs—or cats for that matter—but I can see the appeal.

"You can't be here, Bo. This isn't even my house. Do you know that?"

I pause, taking her in. She's in nothing but her sports bra and running shorts, looking hot as hell. Her bare midriff is flat and sports another dark mole to match the one on her face. Definitely a beauty mark.

It strikes me now that she's too thin, though. Or maybe I'm just seeing the effect of stress on her body. Stress I knew had to be there, but she hid from me before.

"Whose house is it?" I keep my voice down—I have from the beginning.

"It's my aunt's. And I am not going to let you fuck it up with whatever this is."

I perch on the edge of her desk and casually cross one ankle over the other. "So what are you going to do?" I challenge.

I fucking love the blush that crawls up her neck and tinges her cheeks as she probably realizes she sure as hell can't physically make me move.

"I'm going to scream."

I shake my head. "First of all, we both know that's not going to happen, Legs. You're going to keep your mouth shut and tolerate my presence in your life until I decide you're not worth shadowing. Do you know why?"

Her lips thin to a straight line.

"Answer me, Legs."

Her nostrils flare. "Why?" she grits.

"Because I own you now. You ring any warning bells, I will let loose everything I know about you, princess. About the Porsche. And the Mercedes. And your dealings with my brother. I will sing my song like a canary to every fucking cop in this city. And you'll end up in jail, where you really belong."

She has the nerve to cock a hip and toss her hair. "Well, I'm a minor, so jail time is questionable."

Wrong move, sweetheart.

My brother's life has just been ruined, and she's gonna throw that shit at me?

Fuck no.

I slide off the desk and advance on her.

I think she realizes immediately that she went too far, but at that moment, a woman's voice calls out—"Sloane, Rikki! Dinner's ready."

"Coming!" Sloane shouts immediately. She snatches her t-shirt from the floor and yanks it over her head, still maintaining eye contact with me.

I stop my advance, but tension runs through the space between us, aggression radiating from me to her, a repelling push, like a magnet turned the wrong way, shoved back at me.

She doesn't go down easily, I'll give her that.

Not a submissive little thing, this one.

No, she's bold and strong with a warrior's heart. Too bad she's not a wolf. Too bad we're on opposite sides of the line.

"You'd better be gone when I get back," she says, hand on the doorknob.

"Dream on, Legs. I'll be right here." I flick my brows. "Waiting for you."

She flips me the bird as she shuts the door.

Cute. She's damn cute. Beautiful people get away with so much more than ordinary people. My mother used to tell me that as a warning. *You're going to get away with murder out there because you're good-looking. Don't use it to screw people over. Don't screw girls over, Bo.*

Between her and Coach, I've had the respect for women thing drilled into me. Too bad it didn't stick.

Because I feel extremely disrespectful toward Sloane right now.

As soon as she's gone, I start searching her room. Uncovering her secrets.

Because I know this girl conceals more secrets than a priest's confessional. And I want them all.

Lives with her aunt.

Why?

Needs money—a lot of it. Again, why?

Who put her back up against a wall? Why is she afraid of me screwing things up—like she doesn't think she belongs here or something. Did she run away from home? Was she a troublemaker back there?

But why leave her precious Tyler?

Kicked out, then.

But why the money need?

Maybe someone's sick. Dying, even. A parent who can't take care of her, but she feels like she needs to raise money to take care of them. Maybe huge medical bills.

I don't know. It's all conjecture.

The room doesn't hold much, as far as secrets go.

The bulletin board is blank, except for the cross country meet schedule. The desk only has school-related items—pencils, erasers, pens, textbooks, notebooks. Nothing of interest.

I search her backpack and open her wallet. She still has a wad of cash in there. I count it—four hundred and fifty. Not a ton, considering what she must've made on the Porsche deal. Where did the rest of it go?

I check her ID. It's not an Arizona driver's license. It's Michigan. Grosse Pointe. And her eighteenth birthday is this Saturday. She may have been underage when she stole the last two cars, but the next one would carry adult felony charges and penalties.

And that thought puts my teeth on edge.

Despite everything—despite the fact that she's trouble, and she fucked my brother's life over, and my mom and I may never get to see him again, I don't want her ever going to jail. I don't want her to suffer any consequence worse than the ones I bring down on her.

And I do want her safe.

Which means figuring out why she's boosting cars.

Not that I think it's actually that. No, she's stealing for a reason, and I intend to find out what it is.

I check her drawers.

Slow down.

Not because I find anything there, just because I sprout a chub thinking about her without them. And with them. I yank open the drawers until I find her panties. Some are boring. Practical cotton bikini brief shit. The panties she runs in.

But then there's the pretty ones.

For *Tyler*.

Fucking Tyler, who I am going to grind into the goddamn dirt.

That weak human bastard.

She's got lacy ones. Silken ones. A black G-string that gives me a full-on boner.

And then I find it: her vibrator.

It's crazy what it does to me.

A shudder of excitement runs through my entire body. I'm harder than marble now, and I can't seem to turn it off.

There's nothing particularly fancy about the vibe. It's

your basic, plain phallus with a curved tip to hit the G-spot.

Does she hit it? Does she know how? Or is she like one of those girls who has trouble orgasming and can't find her magic buttons?

I'll fucking find them for her.

I'll show her exactly what this wolf knows about pleasing a human teenager. I gained quite a bit of experience last year screwing an ASU cheerleader's brains out for three months.

I drop into her desk chair and turn the vibrator off and on. Every time it rumbles to life, my dick lurches against my jeans

Every time it turns off, I will it down.

I would put it on my balls to feel what it's like, but I'm pretty sure I'd jizz in my pants.

The moon is not even full anymore, and I'm still one stroke from an orgasm. That's what this human does to me.

I breathe down the rumble in my chest. Tell myself not to think about the boyfriend.

The fucking boyfriend.

How can she have a boyfriend?

That asshole back in Grosse Pointe definitely does not deserve a girl this fine. He just doesn't. I know he doesn't.

Girls like this are one in a thousand. Maybe a million. Smart. Athletic. Beautiful. Strong. Fucking devious as hell. What high school student single-handedly starts her own car thieving ring?

It's insane.

I dive back into her backpack, looking for her phone, wondering why I didn't think of it sooner.

It's not there. Does she have it on her? No—impossible. All she was wearing was that thin pair of running shorts. I would've seen a phone sticking out of her pocket, if she had one.

So where?

I spy it plugged in by her bedside table and lunge for it. Scroll through her contacts for Tyler.

He's not fucking there.

What would she call him?

While I have the chance, I download a location tracking app onto her phone and send myself the invite. She might see this and turn it off, but you never know. It could be an easy way to stalk her, if she gives me the slip. Then I scroll through all her contacts, but there are no nicknames. I search by 313, the Grosse Pointe area code. *Nada.*

There are actually very few contacts at all.

Which makes me even more suspicious. Did she delete contacts? Or is the identity a made up one? Maybe she's not actually from Grosse Pointe. Maybe her name isn't Sloane McCormick at all.

Who the fuck is this girl?

~

Sloane

I plow through dinner with my stomach in knots. I just keep hoping Wolf Ridge Boy isn't going to make a sound.

I seriously cannot face my aunt with an explanation of why I have a boy in my room.

I know, it probably wouldn't be the end of the world—but it's absolutely beyond what I can handle right now.

The real problem will be to keep my ever-observant cousin from noticing. Thank God she spends all her time watching Youtube videos with the headphones glued to her head. If it weren't for that, she would've already heard Bo.

I eat half my mac 'n cheese—Rikki's dinner request, obviously—and pick up my plate. "Is it okay if I bring this to my room?"

I don't know why I'm worried about *feeding* Bo.

He's hijacked my personal space in the worst kind of way. And yet I can't help but think how a big guy like him probably eats three times what I do and how hungry he's going to be if he hasn't had dinner.

It's stupid, really.

Aunt Jen considers. "Only if you promise to bring it back down when you're done. I'm not cool with dishes hanging out in bedrooms and attracting ants."

"I promise. I just want to get back to studying. I have a big test."

Not a complete lie.

"Okay, hon. Get to it, then."

My aunt is an elementary school teacher and takes education very seriously. She moved into the Cave Hills district specifically so my little cousin could go to the best schools in Arizona. Never mind that by the time Rikki hits middle school next year, she's already going to get singled out as a have-not. Without the designer clothes and shoes and the parental car-bling, she will not fit in with the Cave Hills kids.

I've managed because I came from money. Before they took everything. Plus, I know how to bluff.

I carry the plate upstairs and check over my shoulder before I open the door.

What I find makes me sorry I had any consideration for the asshole sitting at my desk.

He's holding my freaking vibrator!

"Look what I found." He smirks, holding it up between his thumb and forefinger and waggling it back and forth.

"You *asshole.* Put that away," I grit out between clenched teeth, dropping the plate of mac 'n cheese onto the bedside table.

Damn him. Where does he get off?

"Does Tyler know about this?" He keeps waving it.

I stalk over and try to grab it, but he's too quick, moving it to the side, then up high.

"Does he use it on you, Legs?"

My pussy clenches, even as flames fly out of my ears. I lunge for the vibe, not caring that I plunked my knee right on his thigh to reach up high and grab it.

The perv clamps an arm around the backs of my thighs, his forearm lifting my ass like he's trying to help.

It has the extremely unfortunate effect of getting me horny as hell. Or maybe that's the sight of my B.O.B.

I don't back down, though. If he wants to get up close and personal, I'll go all the way in. I shove my tits in his face and pry the vibrator out of his fingers. I'm pretty sure he only let me because I caught him off guard. The second I have it, I slam it down on the top of his head.

And then I scramble back.

Oops.

I didn't mean to hit him.

That hard.

Or maybe at all.

We both stare at each other in shock. I'm slightly horrified at my own violence—I've never hit anyone in my life.

He looks just as surprised to find I'm capable of it. Or maybe he's really hurt.

"Ouch," he confirms.

"I'm sorry. I shouldn't have hit you with—"

"No you shouldn't have." In a flash, he's up off the chair, divesting me of the vibrator. He tackles me to the bed. "You're in big trouble now, Legs."

Somehow, that sounds more sexy than threatening.

And my body responds with a full on pleasure rush. Heat floods my lady parts. Peaks my nipples.

Somewhere near my right ear, my vibrator roars to life.

"Uh—"

Before I can even assimilate what he's doing, Bo tucks it between my legs, rubbing the shaft back and forth with a sawing motion.

"No—" I reach for it, but he quickly withdraws it and holds it out of reach. He's straddling me—his strong, tree-trunk thick thighs banded around both of mine, pinning me in place. With one hand, he holds my torso down when I try to sit up, still waving the vibrator out of reach.

"You showed me what you can do with it. Now it's my turn."

"Oh no, no, no." My stomach flips. I may be saying no, but I'm creaming my panties, everything molten and wet and absolutely thrilled at this.

His nostrils flare, and his eyes do that silver glint thing. His smile is pure wickedness, and it makes him even more beautiful.

This guy is godlike in every way.

"Here's what we're going to do." He lifts one of his legs, and I start to scramble out, but he grips my hip and flips me to my belly.

"Bo!"

I hear the vibrator drop to the bed, and he pushes a hand into my lower back. Two smacks on my ass—one on each side.

They hurt, and I try to squirm out of his grip, but he's not done. He picks up the vibrator and puts it back between my legs.

Oh God.

It feels. So. Good.

Like I-might-orgasm-right-now good.

It usually takes me forever to get off with the battery operated boyfriend—or B.O.B., as I like to call it. Thirty minutes minimum. But this is like three seconds, and I'm ready to go.

I'm sure it has nothing to do with the extremely hot baller operating it.

The sound that comes out of my lips is full-on embarrassing.

It's a wanton mewl. A signal of how close I am.

Dammit!

I wriggle, humping the bed.

"You need more of this?" He shifts the angle, tucking it up under me so it hits my clit.

I make another wanton sound.

"Fuck." His voice sounds ragged, and that, above all else, makes me feel better. He's turned on, too. I'm not the only one losing control here.

He climbs over me, threading his arms beneath me to

reach the vibrator from my front side, grinding his very hard erection into my ass.

"Like that?" His breath is hot against my ear, and he sounds winded, like I knocked the oxygen right out of him.

"Yeah," I admit, squirming over the hard plastic, rubbing my clit with it through my shorts.

It's so good. My eyes are already rolling back in my head. Waves of heat are washing through me.

"You use it inside or just keep it here?"

"Here," I croak, just as breathless as he is. "Oh God," I whimper.

And then I come. My ass bobs underneath him with the power of the orgasm. I'm dry humping the vibrator and my bed, and I guess him from the back. It's completely embarrassing and infinitely hot.

Bo pants at my neck, grinding into me, grinding me into the bed and vibrator. When I finally finish, he somehow manages to twist his hand enough to turn the vibrator off, but instead of removing it, he nuzzles it around, bringing on another aftershock of clenching and releasing.

He nips my ear. "Now you know the consequences," he murmurs. "Anything else you want to hit me with?"

Another aftershock.

"Get off me!" I complain, and I'm surprised when he instantly complies. In fact, he gets all the way off the bed and backs up to the wall, holding his hands up like he's under arrest.

His usual cocky expression is gone, replaced by something almost sheepish. "Sorry," he says. "No, sorry, not sorry." His lips twist into a grin. "That was too fucking hot for me to be sorry."

I pick up the vibrator and hurl it at him.

He catches it easily and gives me a roguish grin. "Does that mean you want another round?"

CHAPTER 5

I DO FEEL bad if Sloane believes I forced something on her. I mean, I *know* she got off. I scented her arousal before I even got started.

And it literally was the hottest thing I've ever done. I nearly jizzed in my pants.

But if she feels anything other than satisfied by it, then I'm a dick.

"Is that mac 'n cheese?" I ask, to try to bring things back to normalcy.

She scowls at me. "Yeah. I hope it's cold by now."

"Aw, you brought me food, Legs? That was awful sweet of you." I walk across the room to pick up the plate, and she brushes past me on her way to the bathroom.

"Hey." I catch her elbow—softly. No squeeze, no pressure. She stops, and our gazes tangle. Hers is unsure.

Embarrassed. The pad of my thumb brushes lightly over her skin. "You okay?"

I just need to know I didn't leave her feeling violated.

Her lips part, but for once, no quick answer flies out of them.

She's still uncertain.

"Was that rapey? I swear to fate, I would've stopped if you fought me."

"Just shut up, Bo."

I smirk. She's okay. "I'll let you use it on me now."

"Ew." She shoves me away but she's laughing. "You wish."

I nod. "I definitely do wish." I look down at the still-present bulge in my jeans.

She looks, too, and this time she smirks. "Good luck with those blue balls."

I chuckle as she sashays into the bathroom and shuts the door. And now that mac 'n cheese is calling my name.

When she emerges a minute later, I set down the empty plate. Yeah, there's definitely a reason humans call it "wolfing down" food. We definitely wolf. Lots of food.

"How long are you staying?" Sloane demands.

"All night, princess. And I'm going to school with you tomorrow. I'm sure your teachers will be fine with your "out-of-town boyfriend" sitting in on classes, right?" I arch a brow.

She puts her hands on her hips. "If you think you're sleeping in my bed, you are sorely mistaken."

I smirk. "Oh, I'm sleeping on the bed. If you're afraid to sleep near this"— I sweep my hands down my body in a ridiculous beauty queen manner— "then you can take the floor, by all means."

I'm just giving her shit. I will definitely take the floor. I don't know why I like to see how far I can push her. Her mixture of bravado and bluff is full-on entertainment, I guess. Especially when wrapped in that hot package.

She chooses to ignore me and instead flounces to her backpack, pulls out a notebook and throws herself on the bed.

I grab my homework, too, and position myself right beside her on the bed.

She gives me a long, pointed look.

I do *fake innocence* back at her.

She rolls her eyes and directs her focus to her notebook.

We stay that way for over an hour—both of us legit having homework, I guess.

Not that I'm going to school tomorrow. But I can at least do myself the favor of not getting behind.

After a while, I sense her staring at me.

I smirk. "May I help you?"

"Are you seriously staying here all night?"

I nod. "Yep."

She huffs. "Bo, *why*? You can't possibly believe Winslow will show up in the middle of the night *to see me*."

"He might text you. Make contact to meet you to get his share of the money."

"I don't have his money—he was selling the car, remember?"

"Well, to jack another one, then. I'm sticking to you. White on rice."

"You said glue."

I grin. I fucking love giving her shit. And when she gives it back. I love the alpha in her, and honestly, I think if she really didn't want me here, this conversation would be totally different. She'd figure out how to get me out of her house. Or she'd be way more pissed off and tense than she is.

So I'm staying. I'm going to make myself a pain in Sloane's ass because she deserves it after what she did to my family.

"Fine." She gets up and flounces to the bathroom, without shutting the door. I hear her brushing her teeth.

I saunter in behind her. "Borrow your toothbrush, Legs?" I keep my voice low because I know her cousin's bedroom's just on the other side of the door.

"No!" she whisper shouts. But she pulls open a drawer and produces an Oral B still in its package.

I wink as I rip it open then reach for the toothpaste. "Thanks."

She doesn't answer. Instead, she ignores me, heading back to the bedroom, where she shuts off the light and climbs under the covers.

I know because, unlike humans, wolves can see in the dark.

I walk around to the side of her bed and drop to the floor in the small space between the wall and the bed.

The wolf in me thinks I should be at the foot of the bed where I could face an attack from any side—window or door—but the human knows better than to sleep in plain sight, in case her aunt or cousin peek in at some point.

For a few minutes, there's nothing but silence. I know she's not asleep by the rough cadence of her breaths. Like she's alternately holding it, then releasing.

A pillow drops on me.

Smiling, I take it and tuck it under my head.

She tugs the comforter on her bed, so it hangs halfway off the side, sharing it with me.

She's now given me food and comfort.

I'm gonna take it as a fucking welcome wagon. Stay as long as I want. Play her pretend boyfriend. The real asshole can go fuck himself. There's a much better version of him right here in Arizona.

~

SLOANE

MY BODY still buzzes from the orgasm Bo gave me.

It may have been my vibrator, but that was all Bo. I've never achieved those kind of results with the B. O. B.

And the stupid truth I don't want Bo to know is that in addition to not having a real boyfriend, I also haven't had real sex.

As in, with a partner.

No penetration, anyway. I let a few guys eat me.

Didn't orgasm, but it sure felt good.

My sexual experience is another bluff. I was five foot nine by the time I was twelve, with a decent rack. The way I figured it, you can either become one of those girls who slouches around, pretending she doesn't have a full-on woman's body, or you can own it.

So I owned it.

I showed my body off—tastefully, but definitely purposefully. My dad was slightly scandalized, but he didn't interfere. He made a few comments about wishing my mom was alive to "help me through" puberty.

I told him I had it figured out just fine and didn't need any help.

Which was mostly true.

When I went to high school, I became an instant superstar. Guys were attracted to my confidence. Girls wanted to be my best friend. I pretended I had loads of sexual experience, and that let me call the shots.

If I said, *eat me,* guys got on their knees.

Sometimes I returned the favor.

But I didn't do serious relationships, so I never progressed to the next stage of sexual exploration.

Lying here in my dark bedroom with a two hundred plus pound football god lying on the floor beside me has me wishing I already had my V-card punched. Because I don't want this guy to know he's my first.

And I do want him to be my first. He knows what he's doing. My body responds to him.

I respond to him.

If you would've asked me a month ago what my type was, I never would've said some grease-monkey football player from the sticks who hates my guts, but there it is.

I am quickly becoming powerless around his charm.

And he does have charm. He's not a meat-head jock. I don't know how well he does in school, but the guy is smart. He reads people and situations. And he has this cock-sure attitude that makes him both an asshole and wildly attractive.

"Legs." His sexy voice cuts through the darkness, goes straight to my clit, which has been buzzing and pulsing ever since the vibrator incident.

I don't answer. We're not doing pillow talk here. It feels far too vulnerable. Because even though I was fully dressed, I got more intimate with him than I have with any other human being.

"I know you're awake, Legs."

"I'm trying to sleep, Bo."

"What's the money for?"

The room suddenly tilts, then spins. I wasn't prepared for this question. I mean, I should've been. It's part of the reason I'm so defended against Bo Fenton.

That and the fact that he's extremely attractive but seems to hate me.

Although that may be changing.

"Where did the money from the Porsche go? Aside from buying the totaled Mercedes and paying me?"

"None of your business."

Yeah, I know. Real quick. And mature.

But the truth is, it's not. I don't owe him any explanations. I'm sorry his brother got caught, but if Winslow would've let me sell the thing, maybe it wouldn't have happened.

Then again, maybe I'd be sitting in juvie right now, and my innocent cousin would be on her way to fulfill some disgusting pedophile's horrific fantasies.

"I'm gonna find out, Legs. All your secrets. You can't hide them from me."

"You're not."

Even if I wanted to tell him, I wouldn't. Not even if we were besties, and I trusted him with my life. My shit is too dangerous.

"Keep telling yourself that."

There's more silence. I think maybe he's going to let it go, but he says, "Are you in some kind of trouble, Sloane?"

I think it's the first time he's used my real name. I can't

decide if I like it or not. It definitely does something to my chest. Shoots straight in like a dart. Tries to crack me open. There's a sincerity to the way he asked the question, to his use of my name that makes it extra personal. Almost sympathetic.

But I'm not dumb enough to fall into that trap.

Bo Fenton is not my friend.

He's not here to shoulder my burdens. He's not my white knight.

"None of your business, Bo." I repeat in that overly patient sing-song voice.

"Keep it up, and I'm going to climb my giant ass up to that bed and steal all the mattress space, so you're sleeping on the edge with no pillow."

It's a goofy visual and such a soft threat that I chuckle.

I can't see in the dark, but I imagine Bo smiling back. For a guy who hates me, he's starting to get downright flirty.

Can't say I mind it, either.

God help me.

I cannot fall for this guy. Not even for a minute. Not even for pretend.

He doesn't care about me. He's just here to make my life difficult. And even if he did care—and again, he doesn't—I'm not at liberty to form friendships or relationships or any kind of bond that could be exploited by the mafia.

I need to figure out how to get rid of Bo, so I can get on with solving my very serious shit problems.

I need to steal another car and fence it by Monday, or I'm fucked.

CHAPTER 6

o

I'M up before the Cave Hills princess, but I hear movement in the house. Her aunt has already showered and is moving around downstairs.

No sound from the cousin's room.

I get up and quietly pad to the bathroom to pee.

I hardly slept last night because of my raging case of blue balls.

I swear, I almost got up to jack off in the bathroom twenty times, but I suffered through it. I probably should've just let off some steam.

Because now, just the thought of Sloane being in the shower beside me has me harder than stone.

I flush the toilet, and I'm washing my hands when the doorknob from the other bedroom door twists.

Fuck! The cousin!

In a mad scramble, I leap into the bathtub and hide behind the curtain.

A door shuts— the one to Sloane's room.

Fuck.

I hear the sound of her peeing. Then her hand reaches behind the shower curtain and turns the shower on full blast.

I bite down on my yelp of dismay as cold water drenches me. I slept in my jeans and t-shirt last night, and now they're getting soaked. Dammit!

I'm holding my breath, trying to figure out if it's better to rip my clothes and shift into wolf form, so the kid finds a wolf in her shower instead of a very large male stranger when I hear a knock on the door to Sloane's bedroom.

"Rikki?" The door opens and a frantic Sloane peeks behind the curtain on the other side of the shower. She disappears again. "Hey, would you mind if I took a shower first this morning? I promise I'll be super fast. I just feel so gross, I can't stand to wait another minute."

"Uh...okay." Rikki sounds doubtful.

"Thanks. Five minutes—I promise."

"All right."

I hear the door shut, and Sloane rips the curtain back.

I grin at her. The water is warm by now, so not so bad, other than the wet clothes sticking to my body.

Sloane reaches in and grabs a fistful of my t-shirt. "Get out!" she mouths, pulling me forward.

I grin as I allow her to tug me out. I fucking love her getting physical with me. Alpha female all the way. She really shoulda been a wolf.

She yanks a fluffy pink towel from the rack and shoves it at me, then points urgently toward her bedroom.

I laugh silently, walking backward in case she's going to start stripping to get in the shower. Wouldn't want to miss that shit.

She's onto me, though. She flexes her foot and uses it to push me the rest of the way out, then shuts the door in my face.

I strip off my dripping clothes and leave them in a pile on the floor by the bathroom. I don't mind wind-drying them riding my bike, but they really need to be wrung out first, or I'll be wet all day.

Sloane wasn't kidding about keeping her shower short. The water turns off, and I scramble to get the pink towel around my waist before she emerges.

Sadly, she's not in a towel. She comes back wearing the same clothes she went in with, but my undressed status makes her steps stutter.

"Oh! Um…" She glances down at my clothes in a wet heap on the floor, then back up at me. Actually at my chest. Wait—is she ogling my abs?

"Like what you see, Legs?" I murmur in a low voice.

Her skin already glows pink from the shower, but she colors a little more before recovering and tossing her wet head. "You wish, buddy."

I flash her my most wicked grin, but when my cock tries to give her a full salute, I muster enough decency to turn around and saunter to her desk where I plugged my phone into her charger. I keep my back turned and shoot my mom a text letting her know I'm fine and still trying to get in touch with Winslow.

I hear Sloane move quickly behind me, probably trying to get dressed before I turn back around, so I wait until the frantic rustling stops and the sound of her breath slows.

When I look, she's putting on some tunes from an iPhone docking station. Probably to cover any noise I make.

"I'm going downstairs. Feel free to leave any time," she tells me.

I shake my head. "Not happening. Bring food."

"Not happening." She puts extra emphasis on her lip movement since it's more mouthing than speaking, and it makes me want to kiss the hell out of her. It occurs to me that she's had no time to put on makeup or do anything besides comb out her wet hair, and she looks as gorgeous as ever.

She is definitely blessed with good genes. Too bad they aren't of the wolf variety.

I hang out in her bedroom until I hear the cousin go downstairs, and then I carry my clothes into the bathroom to wring them out and put them on. Nothing like trying to yank on wet jeans.

When I return to the bedroom, Sloane is there with a giant bowl of cereal—Life from the looks of it—and two bananas.

"They'll be gone in a few minutes, and you can throw your clothes in the dryer."

"Aw, that's damn sweet of you, Legs."

"It's only because—" She stops and shakes her head. "Actually I don't know why I'm helping you. You are a serious pain in my ass right now."

I nod. "As I intended."

She flips me the bird with her left hand while she shovels a bite of cereal in her mouth.

Cute.

Damn cute.

~

Sloane

Bo waits for me in the parking lot at school when I ride my bike up. He invited me on his motorcycle, but I ignored the offer.

Ignoring his presence is pretty freaking hard to do, though.

Especially now that it's starting to feel like he's more flirting than mad. I really don't know what his game his, but he's damn hard to ignore.

He follows me into the school, straight into my first class—Spanish. Technically, he's supposed to sign in at the office, but I'm not going to hold his hand for this. Frankly, I'm hoping he gets kicked out.

"Who is this?" Señorita Allen asks in surprise. I'm pretty sure she's ogling Bo's biceps. Which, why wouldn't she, right? They're a work of art.

"I'm her boyfriend Tyler, visiting from Michigan." He sticks his hand out and flashes a panty-melting smile.

Señorita Allen falls for it. In fact, she invites the dude who normally sits next to me to take the seat in the back, so "Tyler" can sit beside me.

Lucky me.

He sits up straight, either listening attentively, or watching me with exaggerated attention, like he's a love-sick dog.

It's freaking embarrassing, and I'm ready to throat-punch him by the time the bell rings for my next class.

"Hey, there he is," Teri gushes, catching sight of us in the hallway. "So fun you could come to school, Tyler!"

"Isn't it though?" he gushes right back. "I wouldn't miss a minute of time with my girl. She's my whole world." He puts his fist over his chest.

Teri looks uncertain, like she can't decide if he's making fun of her or being serious.

I roll my eyes and smack his chest with the back of my hand. "He's being a dork. Ignore him!"

She bursts into a peal of giggles. "Hilarious. See you guys at lunch!"

"Can't wait!" Bo calls out in a high pitched voice.

I smack him again.

He catches my wrist and with a quick tug pulls me against his solid chest. We're in the middle of the hallway, but the crowd of students parts around us. I hear giggles and feel the curious stares as they pass.

"Careful, Legs," he rumbles. "Remember your punishment for hitting me?"

I try to pull away, but he holds my wrist fast, slowly bringing my fingers to his lips and kissing one knuckle, then the next.

I'm trying not to think of it—I really am—but in my mind, he's on top of me again, and this time he's pressing my own fingers over my clit, talking dirty in my ear. Making me come over and over again.

I might have been pissed at him over what he did yesterday. It was definitely as humiliating as it was exciting. But he knew he crossed the line, and he checked in with me. So I'm good. And yes, I get shivers every time I think about it happening again.

And even though my first priority needs to be getting rid of this guy, I definitely *do* want it to happen again.

So I answer, "I'll take my chances, Muscles."

He bites my knuckles—a quick nip—then releases my hand with a grin. As we resume the walk down the hall, I'm pretty sure he has to adjust his junk because I just made him hard.

Two can play at this game.

And I always play to win.

Bo

CAVE HILLS CLASSES aren't quite as boring as Wolf Ridge. They're harder, for sure. I can see why it's a top rated public high school. The teachers are entertaining and smart. They are relaxed with the kids, who don't give them shit. Totally different culture.

I emailed Wolf Ridge High this morning from my mom's account to say that I needed to stay home to deal with some family business. Considering how small Wolf Ridge is and how fast gossip travels, the attendance clerk at school will assume that means I'm dealing with the Winslow problem and cut me some slack.

I know the other alpha-holes would sneer at my admiration of Cave Hills, and part of me wants to sneer too. These kids are so sheltered, they don't know how easy they've got it. All they have to do is work hard at school, and life gets handed to them on a platter. They're not working jobs on the side, dealing with shit like alcoholic parents or abuse.

Then again, maybe they are. Sloane must have some pretty big problems, or she wouldn't be stealing cars.

At lunchtime, Sloane leads me around to the back of a building to eat her lunch.

"Are we hiding?" I ask.

She gives me a death glare. "Obviously."

"You don't want to show off your hot boyfriend?" I make a show of flexing my arm and popping my muscles.

She rolls her eyes.

"Oh, there you two are!" Sloane's eager beaver friend Teri pops around the corner with Samantha. When she sees Sloane's lack of excitement, she covers her mouth. "Oh my God, did you guys want some private time? I'm sorry!"

I scoot closer to Sloane on the grass and pick her up to sit on my lap. "Yeah, we're going to do it right here in the grass," I boast.

"Will you get off!" Sloane scrambles off my lap and bats at me again while her friends laugh.

"I'm trying to."

She slaps me again. I catch her hand and bring it to my mouth, making a big show of kissing each finger while she wrestles me the whole time to take it back.

Her friends clearly decide they're not intruding because they plop down on the grass with us.

"So are you staying with Sloane? At her aunt's place?" Samantha asks.

"Yep," I answer immediately, at the same time Sloane says *no*.

They glance from one to the other of us. "Well, which is it?"

I give a wicked grin. "I'm staying there, but her aunt doesn't know. I crawled in her window last night." I waggle my brows like we're the naughtiest little high school sweethearts imaginable.

Sloane blushes.

"Well, we won't tell." Samantha sounds like she's reprimanding Sloane. Probably offended she hadn't been in on the truth.

They can't be that tight yet, though, or Sloane would've already told them I'm not the real boyfriend.

Why didn't she? That doesn't really add up. If she doesn't want me around, why not just deny it from the beginning?

Unless…

There is no Tyler.

But why would she have a made up boyfriend?

Dude, this girl is so shady, it's hard to know what's truth and what's lie.

It's hard to stay hardened against her, though, when she does things like pack me a lunch. She hands me two neatly wrapped peanut butter and jelly sandwiches. "Hope you don't have a peanut allergy."

"Wouldn't you know if he did?" Samantha asked. These Cave Hills kids are too bright for their own good.

Sloane takes a bite of her sandwich. "Totally. I'm just kidding. I know he's good." She shoots me glance, and I confirm with a giant bite of the sandwich.

"Mmm, this is delicious. And you're a peach."

She rolls her eyes.

"So, tell me about Sloane's life at Cave Hills. She's the track star, of course."

"Definitely. She's taken first at every meet so far. We might have a chance at State this year," Samantha says.

"Yeah right, like Wolf Ridge High would ever give up their reign."

I open my mouth, about to say something honest, like "you never know"—because we do have to lose sometimes, or it would look strange—until I remember I'm from out of town. "And what else? You two are her besties?"

"Will you stop grilling my friends? You already know all this stuff."

I flash my flirty grin at the girls. "I like to hear it from them."

Teri offers, "It's a good thing you came because she's probably going to win Homecoming Queen, and she wasn't even going to go."

That's right. Homecoming.

And I'm her date.

"When is that?"

Teri narrows her eyes. "Tonight," she says with a what-the-hell-is-wrong-with-you expression.

Tonight. Right. Fuck—I have a football game.

I wink, though. "I know, I meant what time?"

"Seven," Teri and Samatha say at once.

Seven. That might work. The game is at four. If Coach lets me play, I still have time afterwards to shower, put on a tie and get back to Cave Hills. Might be a little late, but that's fashionable.

"We don't need to go," Sloane attempts.

"Of course we do, *babycakes.*" I reach over and thumb

some peanut butter from the corner of her lips, loving playing the doting boyfriend role because it pisses her off. "That's the whole reason I'm here. And you might get crowned queen. And here I just thought you were a princess."

She elbows me.

I catch her around the waist and pull her back on my lap as punishment. When she struggles, I tickle her, then open my knees to trap her in the hole between them, so I can cage her with legs and arms.

It's way too intimate, and I know that fucking drives her crazy.

I like torturing her.

I also like the way she feels in my arms. Her scent all up in my nostrils, her soft skin under my hands.

I normally don't have a thing for humans, but I could honestly say a girl like this one would be worth making an exception for.

Too bad I don't trust her as far as I can throw her.

And she hates me.

And she destroyed my family.

CHAPTER 7

loane

I TOLD Bo we're not going to Homecoming.

Not that I believe it will do any good.

When that guy decides something, he doesn't bend. He left after lunch saying he had a football game but he'd be back to pick me up for the dance.

I told him not to come.

He told me to look sharp.

So here I am, using a curling iron on my hair and wearing last year's Homecoming dress—a little strappy black number, while my cousin looks on.

"So *who* is your date?" she asks for the fifth time.

"Just a guy from school," I say.

"I know, but what's his name?"

Even that question is tricky. I have too many lies going now. I didn't tell my aunt and cousin I had a made up boyfriend, so they don't know about the fictitious Tyler. But if I tell her his name is Bo, and then Teri and Samantha hear it… sigh.

This is all getting ridiculous.

And is a total distraction from what I need to be focused on—survival.

Still, Rikki's enthusiasm for me is slightly infectious. And one tiny part of me is slightly excited to be taken to a dance by my very drool-worthy date.

If nothing else, he's a great fake boyfriend. Big. Muscly, and pretend-attentive. I know he's mocking me the whole time, but sometimes my mind slips to wondering if that's how he'd really be with a girlfriend.

I doubt it—and I wouldn't want that doting boyfriend thing. But I do want to know what he'd really be like.

Is real boyfriend Bo like the guy in my room last night —the one who asked if I was okay after pushing me too far?

What would he be like with a real girlfriend? Would he be sweet when he took her V-card?

Ugh! Why am I thinking about that?

Even if I do have sex with him, I'm not going to let him know I'm a virgin.

"His name is Bo." I go for the truth. I've veered too far from it lately, and it only comes back to bite me.

"Do you like him?"

I apply a second coat of mascara. "Um… sometimes. Not really. Yeah."

She gives a quizzical look. "What does that mean, exactly?"

I laugh. "He's super hot, but he knows it. And he can be a jerk."

"But he asked you to Homecoming? Or you asked him?"

"Well...I guess he asked me." Does forcing me count as asking?

Sophie barks, and Rikki runs to the window in my room. "Oh wow. Does he drive a fancy car?"

"No." I gulp, thinking it must be the mafia guys, but then I see the car she's referring to. It's a beautifully restored old convertible Mustang in shiny red. "Oh wait—yeah, that must be him." The guy works at a body shop. He'd probably have access to a car like that.

The doorbell rings, and Rikki tears down the stairs to answer. Sophie's barking stops and turns to a whine of submissive glee when the door opens.

It's weird the power he has over that dog.

Downright bizarre.

My heart's pumping fast, but it's probably just from the mafia scare. Not because I'm excited or nervous about being picked up for a dance. That's stupid.

Downstairs, I hear Aunt Jen and Rikki talking and the deep rumble of Bo's voice in reply.

Damn. Maybe I am excited because it does something flippy to my stomach.

I slip on a pair of stilettos and hurriedly throw my essentials in an evening purse.

When I come down the stairs, Bo stops speaking mid-sentence. His eyes glint silver to match his grey tie. If I thought the jock from Wolf Ridge couldn't clean up or would look awkward in dress clothes, I was sorely mistaken. If I'm totally honest, I'll admit I half expected him to show up in a greasy t-shirt and jeans just to embarrass me at the dance.

But no. He looks like a million bucks. And is totally at ease in a crisp white button down with a jacket and tie. Like a *GQ* model. Or a celebrity.

Very fuckable.

And I've never had that thought about a guy before in my life.

"Oh, sugar. You're showing your legs." He sounds almost pained, but the appreciation is obvious in his expression.

Maybe I did pick this dress for him, at least subconsciously. It's a straight sheath that hits mid-thigh without looking skanky. On a shorter girl it might make her legs look short or chunky, but I have long legs, so I can pull it off.

Aunt Jen stiffens at his remark. I don't think she's prepared to deal with sexual innuendos, especially in front of Rikki.

Charmer that he is, though, Bo catches himself. "Sorry, ma'am."

Ma'am? Seriously? Are we in the South? Once more, I didn't know he had it in him, but Bo Fenton is full of surprises.

"I promise to be completely respectful with Sloane. What time do you want her home?"

My aunt is duly charmed. And a little flustered because I don't have a curfew, and that isn't something she's had to deal with for Rikki yet. "Oh, ah, what time is the dance over?"

"We'll be back by eleven," I say at the same time she warbles "Midnight is fine."

"Midnight it is." Bo winks.

Seriously—who winks? This guy with his pirate smile.

He reaches his hand out for mine. I want to ignore the gesture, but Rikki and Aunt Jen are looking on, smiling, so I put my palm in his.

His calloused hand is large and rough. I hate the way it makes butterfly wings flap in my belly. I really don't need this kind of distraction in my life right now.

Especially not from a guy set on wrecking my heart.

His smile mocks me as we walk out, but he gives my hand a squeeze before he lets me shake off his grip. He opens the door for me, like a gentleman.

Again, I'm surprised that he has manners.

"Nice wheels."

"They're Winslow's. So we'll probably get pulled over since the manhunt is still on. You might want to hold back on the drinking."

I shoot him a disgusted look. "I'm not going to be drinking!"

He shrugs. "You could. I'm driving. And I'm sure *Tyler* would take good care of his girlfriend if she got drunk."

The mention of Tyler makes my stomach tighten.

He gives me a searching look as he slides in the driver's seat. "There is no Tyler, is there?"

The stone in my stomach drops out completely with a whoosh. I'm left breathless.

For some reason, his guess shakes my foundation. It was a stupid lie, it hardly matters, but if he guessed this truth, what else will he deduce?

"I checked your phone contacts," he admits, probably noting how stunned I am.

I still can't speak. Can't answer. I tuck my hands between my legs because for some reason, they are trembling. I don't know why I suddenly feel so exposed, but I do.

Maybe I was counting on Tyler to keep the distance between me and this beautiful, dangerous, vengeful guy.

Bo starts the car, but he doesn't take his focus off me. "Why did you make him up?"

I swallow around the band tightening my vocal cords. "To keep the guys off me," I admit. My voice comes out scratchy.

"Why?"

I shake my head. I'm still trembly. "I didn't want the attention. Or the distraction." *Or anyone to get killed.*

His blue gaze bores into the side of my head for a moment longer, and then he finally looks through the windshield and puts the Mustang in gear. "I'm glad," he says without looking my way.

I almost don't want to ask what he's glad about, but I do. "Why?"

"I was pretty much going to kill the fucker if he ever showed up here for real."

A flood of heat washes through me, and my lady parts tingle. "That's ridiculous." I hate how shaky my voice sounds.

He shrugs, still not looking. Like he's not sure he should've admitted it.

"I'm just saying. Tyler's lucky he doesn't exist."

A puff of laughter escapes my lips. "You are one crazy son of a bitch, Bo."

"That is true," he says, like he's proud of it.

We ride in silence for a moment, and then I remember to ask, "How was your game?"

"We won."

"And they let you play? I thought you have to be at school on the day of a meet or game in order to participate."

"Coach busted my balls pretty hard, but he let me play. He knows what went down with Winslow." He slides a glance over my way, and guilt makes my stomach tighten again.

"I'm sorry."

It's the first time I've said it. Or if I said it before, this is the first time I mean it. I never liked Winslow—he scared the crap out of me, and I don't actually think he was that nice of a guy. But I am starting to feel something for Bo. And he seemed to know from the beginning this wouldn't end well for his brother. He tried to get me to stay away.

I ignored him.

And while I can't believe his getting caught is actually my fault—I mean, Winslow is an adult and made his own decisions—I do feel bad that Bo lost his brother over this.

Just another casualty in my shit show.

Another reason for me to shake Bo out of my hair for good before he gets hurt even more.

"Did Cave Hills play their Homecoming game today? Oh hey—am I taking the Homecoming Queen?"

"No, the game was last night, and they won't announce it until the dance."

"And you really weren't going to go?"

I grip the door handle, thinking about why things like Homecoming royalty don't mean anything to me. "No."

Bo shoots another one of those searching glances my way. "Because you're in some kind of trouble."

It's a statement, not a question. And once again, I feel exposed.

"Maybe this shit just doesn't matter to me."

"Maybe." His tone suggests how unlikely that answer is.

We get to the dance, and I pay for us to get in, mainly because I doubt Bo has much money, and I still have a little bit I saved from the sale of the Porsche.

Bo walks in like he owns the place, which works, because that's the way I usually carry myself, too. I'm not used to sharing the limelight with my date, though. He greets Teri and Sam like they're long-lost friends, shakes hands with their dates—both nice but slightly gangly guys from the cross-country team.

He threads his fingers through mine and leads me through the crowd. Everyone turns to watch us. We're both tall and good-looking and carry ourselves like we're the shit.

Aw, screw it. I decide to go with the ruse. It's the best way not to let Bo get under my skin. I pull him straight out to the dance floor and lambada my body right up against his.

He lets out an animalistic growl and bands an arm around my waist.

Oh God. I love it—way too much. His body is solid muscle, and he knows how to move. He insinuates his thigh between mine, pulling me against him, so I grind down on it.

Dang. We've been here five minutes, and I'm already primed for sex.

How freaking cliche would it be if I lost my virginity on prom night? I mean Homecoming, but same difference—a school dance.

~

Bo

I'M high on the scent of Sloane's arousal.

She's sending all the signals, but I'm pretty sure it's a ruse. Beating me at my own game.

I rock my hips to the music, holding her body close to mine, trying to figure out if her panties are damp where she's grinding on my leg.

I want to fuck her senseless.

That part isn't new.

The part I'm really fighting right now is the desire to kiss her. I'm trying to figure out what she would do. Whether I play it off as more torture, meant to embarrass her in front of her school, to punish her for her lies, or whether I kiss her for real.

The way I want to.

Unfortunately, or maybe fortunately, my debate is interrupted by the call for homecoming royalty to take the stage.

When they call Sloane's name, I cup the back of her head and pull her mouth up to mine. "Make me proud, princess."

It's punishment, and it doesn't taste nearly as sweet as the claiming I was imagining.

In fact, it tastes a little bitter, especially the way she shoves away from me and doesn't look back. She sashays to the stage and stands up there with the other senior class nominees. The superior way she holds herself on stage tells me she can't wait to get off it.

They announce and crown the royalty from lower classmen up, saving the seniors for last. I'm not a bit surprised when her name is called as queen. I put my fingers in my mouth and give a loud whistle that makes everyone look my way. I do mock adoration and clap with the rest of them while Sloane accepts the crown with a fake smile and a shouted *thank you*.

I feel like a complete jackass when she leaves the stage and beelines it away from me, toward the bathrooms.

~

Sloane

I DUCK into the bathroom stall and lean my back against the door with an exhale.

It's all just so empty. When I got to Cave Hills High, I held my head high, tossed my hair and played the part I knew so well. I didn't want anyone to know about my past, so I became their queen.

But now I'm a little queasy after being on stage. I don't want this damn crown. Sure, I loved getting crowned Homecoming royalty every year of high school in Grosse Pointe, but that feels like a million and a half years ago.

I was a different person then. The wealthy but ignored princess of a stock broker. Crowns and popularity helped fill the void left by an empty home life.

Now, I know it's all bullshit. I knew what to say and how to act to win their esteem. I'm a little standoffish, a lot better-than-thou, and I have all the right clothes and accessories, minus the car. And of course, I'm pretty. I guess that's enough to win me homecoming queen.

No one out there is a real friend. No one has any idea of who the real Sloane McCormick is. The girl who pretty much always suffered from imposter syndrome. Never felt like she deserved the space she takes up. They'd turn on me in a heartbeat if they knew who my father was. What he did. What I've done to try to save my ass.

And having Bo out there witnessing it all somehow makes me feel like all the cracks in my armor show. Before, no one looked too closely.

But he does. He sees way too much, that guy. And I know he's mocking me every step of the way.

And yet, the crazy part is how addictive his attention is, too. I'm running from it, but part of me can't wait to go out there and dance with him again. Look into that handsome face and keep flipping him the bird.

So I exit the stall, put on fresh lipgloss and head back out. I find Bo sitting with my friends at one of the tables, drinking punch and ice waters and laughing. I pull out a chair, but Bo tugs me onto his lap, his strong arm curling around my waist.

This is pretend. He's trying to make me uncomfortable, so like on the dance floor, my best solution is to go with it. I loop an arm around his strong shoulders, lean in and bite his ear. Kinda hard.

His arm tightens around my waist. "Careful," he murmurs. "Or I'll be punishing you later." His hand trails up my leg. He shifts his legs—and mine on top of his—so they're under the table, hidden by the tablecloth. Then he slides his calloused palm right up my inner thigh.

I squeeze my legs together to stop its ascent before he hits the apex.

"Mmm," he rumbles and nips my shoulder. "I think Tyler would definitely be at third base, don't you?" His wicked voice is a murmur against my skin. Too quiet for my friends to hear. Enough to set my panties on fire.

I shift slightly on his lap, and he groans, letting me know his dick is hard against my ass.

"Come on, Legs. Open those sweet thighs just a little more."

I don't want to. Well, that's not true—I desperately want to. That's the problem. I shouldn't, though. Bo is here to taunt me, and this torture just may be my undoing.

And I can't help myself.

My thighs ease apart, just a little more, and his fingers slide higher, brushing the gusset of my panties.

I wore a sexy thong—G-string, actually. Obviously some part of me knew I'd be letting this baller under my skirt tonight.

He takes his time, teasing me with the lightest feather touch on the silk of my panties. It has the effect of sensitizing every part of my body. Causing me to lean into the sensation, turn every receptor on.

Then he slides his finger underneath.

I close my lips around my gasp. My pelvic floor lifts and squeezes at the same time my thighs fall open wide for him.

"That's it, sugar. Open for me."

My nipples burn against my dress, core heats. And I'm wet. Embarrassingly wet. He initiates a slow exploration of my swollen lady parts, and I have to work to keep from panting. To keep from moaning. Every part of it feels wonderful.

He kisses my neck and probes my entrance with his finger. When I tighten, he moves away, exploring my clit, instead, until my breath gets labored, and I'm writhing on his lap. Then he gives it a tap, like a little spank, and pulls his fingers out, bringing them to his mouth to lick.

I grab his wrist and try to pull it down, horrified someone might see and guess what he's been doing, but he's really freaking strong. I don't even budge him. He smiles around his fingers at me, eyes looking silver in the dim light.

"I definitely want more of that," he says.

I scramble off his lap, way too horny for a high school dance. "I have to go to the bathroom."

"You can run, but you can't hide." Bo murmurs, his pirate smile in full bloom, eyes winking with mischief.

Damn him for being so attractive.

Damn him for getting under my skin.

I escape before he does any more damage.

Bo

I HAVE to stay in my seat for a minute until I can get my cockstand under control. Then I head out the back doors for some air. I pull out my phone and check for any messages from Winslow.

"Hey, isn't that guy one of the Wolf Ridge ballers?"

Shit.

It's a football player from Cave Hills.

What are the chances of me being recognized here? We're in helmets and matching jerseys. I shouldn't be that easy to pick out.

"Yeah, it is."

"He came with Sloane McCormick," another helpful teammate offers.

"No shit."

The team strolls over, their alpha—because humans have alphas, too, even if they don't understand pack dynamics—in the lead.

I sense the aggression in them right away, and my wolf snarls, but I hold him down.

This is one of those instances Coach lectures us over and over about. We don't fight humans. It doesn't matter how stupid or annoying they are. We have to suppress the urge to show our dominance.

Because, of course, we would dominate in any fight. No human could stand a chance against our superior strength.

If I were smart, I would turn around and walk into the school right now.

Find Sloane. Ask her if she wants to go home.

But my wolf won't let me tuck tail and run. I may not be able to fight, but I sure as hell can't hide.

I lean against the brick wall and watch them come at me, their chests puffed for posturing. "What's up, assholes?"

Their leader grabs a fistful of my shirt and bangs me against the wall.

I have to concentrate to let my muscles go slack. Not to give into the instinct to swing at him.

"Really? You're calling us assholes? I think you're on our turf, tonight."

"Nah. We own the goddamn state, dickwad. It's all my turf." It's stupid, I know. Coach Jamison would have my balls for goading him, but I can't help myself. These guys are such clowns, strutting around like peacocks.

He swings, and I duck. His friends move in fast, though. They pin my arms while he beats on my ribs a few times. I could throw them off me. It would be so easy. I could crush all three of these little fuckers, but this is one of those moments I take one for the pack.

We can't always come out on top—the human world would get suspicious.

He clocks me in the face, and my mouth fills with blood. Either a tooth got knocked out or went through my lip. It doesn't matter—I'll heal within an hour or two.

What does matter, though—what bothers the fuck out of me—is Sloane choosing that moment to walk out.

I shove one of the guys off me to free my right arm, even as I try to talk myself down.

I'm saved from having to punch one of them, though, when Sloane marches over, yelling, "Get. Off. My. Boyfriend."

My muscles go loose again, and I grin like an idiot.

The alpha holes will have a heyday with this when I tell them.

Saved by a girl.

A human girl.

The ugly-ass leader's lip curls with fury. "*This* is your boyfriend?" He throws another punch, but I dodge. "You said you had a boyfriend back in Detroit."

"I did. Until I met Bo."

Huh.

I don't know what she's playing at, but I'm enjoying the hell out of it. She's claiming me as a boyfriend now?

She must really not like this asshole.

He throws another punch, and I start to dodge, but at the last moment, change my mind and let it fall. It hits my jaw.

"Stop it!" Sloane screams. The genuine alarm in her voice gets my wolf riled up like he needs to protect her. Of course, it's me she's screaming over. "Let him go!"

"Why would you go out with this guy?" He shoves me, which throws off the balance of his friend pinning my arm. "Don't you know he's from Wolf Ridge?"

Sloane's dislike is evident now. She glares at the guy with pure disgust. "I'm sure that means something to you, but you forget, I'm not from around here. It means absolutely nothing to me."

"They're like ignorant hillbillies," his teammate jumps in to explain. "Inbred white trash who are dumb as rocks but can take a tackle. All they know how to do is play sports, but not a single one of them ever goes to college."

I don't punch him. It would be too easy. Instead I just shake out of his grip and walk cockily to Sloane.

"The only one showing their ignorance right now is you, Brian," Sloane throws back, reaching for my hand. She leads me away from the building, toward the parking lot.

I let her lead until we turn the corner, and then I put my arm around her shoulders like I need help. She just saw me get my ass beat. I have to at least act a little hurt.

"Oh God, are you okay?"

I give her a wide grin. I still taste blood in my mouth,

so it's probably a colorful one.

"What are you smiling at?"

"You, rescuing *me*."

"Don't think it means I like you."

I unlock the passenger side door to Winslow's Mustang. "I think you do, Legs."

After she gets in, I walk around and start the car. Its early still—there's time to take her out somewhere. And that idea appeals to me, but not as much as getting her home, considering I plan on spending the night in her bedroom again.

And not on the floor.

I pull out, and she yanks off her crown, tosses it on the dash, then fiddles with the ancient radio in the car until she picks up a station.

I park in front of her aunt's townhouse and turn off the car.

"You don't have to walk me to the door."

"Oh, but I do. I promised your aunt I'd be respectful."

She snorts as she slides out of the car and shuts the door, booking it to the townhouse like she can't wait to get rid of me.

I have to hustle to catch up, but my legs are longer. I reach past and catch the door knob before she does. "What, no kiss?"

"Fuck no." She gives me a shove.

I want the kiss, though. I want it badly. Time to stop being a dick.

I slide my hand under her hair. "Just one," I coax. "I'll make it good."

She hesitates, uncertainty glinting in her copper-brown eyes. She wants it, too. She just doesn't trust me.

I lower my head. Brush my lips across hers, testing. She doesn't pull away. I make more contact, but it's still light.

She kisses back, just a little.

I snake my arm around her waist and deepen the kiss. Everything about it feels good.

Right.

The way she tastes. The way her body fits against mine. The tentative way she gives herself to me.

I press her back against the door and go in for the kill. Sweep my tongue between her lips. Drop my hand to her ass.

She softens even more. Lets me.

"You taste like blood," she murmurs when I let her up for air.

I lift my chin toward her window upstairs. "Then let me in, and I'll brush my teeth."

She considers me with heavy-lidded eyes, then opens the door and slips inside.

I take it as a *yes* and barely refrain from a fist pump as I walk to the Mustang to park it somewhere nearby where her aunt won't see.

I lose the tie and jacket in the car and grab my backpack with a change of clothes and my phone charger and toss in her crown from the dash. Then I slip back through the darkness and swing soundlessly up to the porch roof.

Sloane stands in the open window, watching my approach. "You make that look easy."

I shrug and pop off the screen to slip through. "It is easy." *Because I have superhuman strength.* But I'll let her be impressed, just this once.

She has music playing—probably to block out any sound I make.

I dig out and hand her the crown, biting back every princess comment that comes to mind. Instead, I drop my backpack and hook my index finger behind the spaghetti strap of her black dress. "You were undeniably the queen tonight."

She chuffs, brushing off the compliment but allowing my touch. She points at the blood splattered on my white shirt. "I'm sorry the guys at my school are such jerks."

"Nah, I'm good. I might have egged them on a bit."

"When it's three to one? How smart is that?"

I shrug. The hole in my lip is already half-healed, but she wouldn't know that. "You're right. It was stupid." I grin and head to the bathroom to brush the taste of iron out of my mouth, so she'll kiss me again.

When I come back, I find she hasn't moved. She's just standing there, watching me.

Considering.

No, she's nervous.

I don't know why I didn't pick it up before, but I do now. When I listen close, I hear her heartbeat pumping faster than it should. Smell the tinge of fear in her scent, mingled with arousal.

Sloane McCormick—the gorgeous, sex-drenched goddess among humans—is nervous with a guy? With me?

I'd be flattered, except I don't think it's about me.

She's been pretty damn comfortable with me from the start. We don't try to impress each other—we give each other shit.

I stalk over to her, grab the back of her head and slam my lips down on hers.

A shudder runs through her, and then she slowly

cracks open. She steps into the space between us, places her hands on my ribs.

"Hey, beautiful," I say softly when we break the kiss. I stroke her cheek with my thumb. "Is this your first time?"

She stiffens, her eyes flying to mine.

"Don't be nervous. I'll make it good—I promise." I hook my forearm under her ass and lift her to straddle my waist, walking a few steps forward to lower her on the bed.

Vulnerability shows on her face, and it makes me want to slay dragons for her.

"How did you know?"

I nip her inner thigh as I slide down to position my head between her legs. "I put it together."

I'm waiting for a protest of any kind, but all I sense is relief. She drops her head back on the bed and lets me push her thighs wide.

She's wearing a pair of panties I saw in her drawer—a black satin G-string that's easy to push to the side. Her pussy's shaved bare.

For me.

I lick into her, hooking her thighs over my shoulders and molding my hands around her ass. When she jacks her hips off the bed, I delve in deeper, penetrating her with my tongue, lapping at her juices. I investigate her princess bits until I find her clit. It swells when I pull back the hood and tongue it, and she clamps her knees around my ears.

I thrash her with my tongue, swirling it around until her clit gets engorged enough for me to suck. And then affix my lips over it and pull while I slide a finger inside her.

She arches up, squeezing my finger and lets out a

broken moan. "Take off your clothes, Muscles," she orders.

I give her a smirk. "You think you're calling the shots tonight, queeny?"

She nods. "I'm definitely calling the shots." Her voice is husky and rich. It gets me harder than stone.

I slide my finger out.

All right, yeah. I'll let her call the shots. It's her show. But I pull her panties with me as I back off the bed.

She helps me, watching with heavy-lidded eyes. "Off," she mouths.

"I heard you, princess." I unbutton my shirt and shrug out of it, then lose the white undershirt. I leave on the dog tags because I never remove them.

She watches as I unbuckle my belt and free my erection. I do a quick search for a condom in my pocket as I step out of the pants and rip the package open.

It occurs to me she could blue-ball me again. Get me standing here with my dick in my hand and then tell me to fuck off.

But one look at her face tells me that won't happen. Her cheeks are flushed, eyes glassy. She wants this.

I roll the condom on, keeping my gaze locked on hers. The zipper's on the side of her dress, and I tug it down, then easily slip the sheath off her, so she's naked.

She's as porn-ready and beautiful as I imagined. Her tits are firm as apples with nipples that tilt up. Her belly is flat—there's that beauty mark I noticed last night.

"You want the vibrator again?"

It's shocking how much different I feel about it than I did last night. Now that I know there's no boyfriend. And she's not nearly as experienced as she pretends.

She shakes her head and eyes my dick. "I want that."

I can't stop the mile wide grin from stretching across my face. "Yeah?"

I crawl over her. "You think you can handle this?" I grip my cock and give it a shake. I'm teasing her because I know it will put her at ease. She's comfortable when there's a challenge on the table.

"Please, you're not that big."

I smirk. "Famous last words."

She tries to squeeze her knees closed. "Wait, wait, wait."

Of course, I do.

"You're actually huge. Do we need some lube?"

I drag the head of my sheathed cock through her copious juices. "Do we, sugar? You feel pretty wet to me. But I'm happy to get slippery if you have some."

"Never mind. Just try it."

She's nervous again. I want to get her past it, so she can get off.

I pin both her wrists above her head with one hand and grip my cock with the other, lining it up with her entrance. I rock slowly, applying a little pressure until the tip slips in. Then a little more. She's tight, but wet, and I fit. I don't feel any barrier. A few more gentle thrusts, and I'm in, fully seated, stretching her wide. I stay deep and let her adjust.

"You okay?"

She nods. She doesn't look like she's in pain, but she doesn't look particularly pleasured, either.

I pull out. "Come here." I drop to my back beside her. "You ride. You're the queen tonight. Take what you need."

She scrambles up—no hesitation. I definitely know this girl. I may not have all her secrets yet, but I know her.

~

Sloane

I DON'T KNOW why I was so against Bo knowing I'm a virgin. He's a sweetheart in bed. Lying back, his Adonis-like body on full display, he's every bit the gentleman. Gone is the dickish asshole trying to make my life miserable.

Now he's all consideration and patience. I lean over to turn up the radio a little more, just in case, then throw a leg over his waist and rise up to position myself over his cock. He holds it firm for me as I slowly lower myself down on it.

So. Good.

I start to rock my hips. He helps me, gripping my ass with his large palms. We find a rhythm, and I ride it.

Then I need more. I grab his wrists and pin them down beside his head. He gives me that pirate smile. We both know I'd lose any real wrestling match with him, but he'll let me play. Let me pretend I have the upper hand for once in our rocky relationship. I pick up my speed, rubbing my clit forward and back as I move over him.

It's incredible. I want more. All of it.

"You want me to touch you, princess? Let me touch you."

I'm not sure what exactly he means, but I release his wrists. He brings his thumb to my clit and starts rubbing. With the other hand, he reaches behind and presses the pad of one of his fingers against my anus.

I bite back a shriek at the sudden onslaught of attention. Of sensation. I'm bucking, riding him like he's a bronco. It's all too much—the loss of control, panic at the orgasm hurtling toward me. I topple sideways as it rips through me.

Bo is a prince because he follows me over, staying inside me, taking over the work of thrusting while he still rubs my clit. Wave after glorious wave of pleasure rolls through me as I smother my cries and gasps in the bedcover.

Bo pushes one of my knees up toward my chest and goes for his finish, hammering into me in my twisted, sideways position.

I watch him, mind blown with my own orgasm. Mind blown at the sight of him—this full grown spectacular specimen of malehood, all ripped muscles and power. If he was respectful before, it's gone now.

Now he's nothing but pure, animal need. I got mine, and now he's after his. And he's taking it. A more timid girl would be frightened by this display. The intensity. The loss of control. There'd be no stopping him now, if I wanted to. But I definitely don't want to. I'm in awe, fascinated by his unapologetic virility.

His face contorts, as if in pain, and then he slams home and stays, eyes squeezed shut.

But a second later, his eyes fly open and find my face. "Shit, are you okay? Was I too rough?"

I shake my head. He was, but I'd never tell him, and not out of pride this time. Because I learned something about myself: I like it rough. I'm going to be sore—I already am sore, but holy hell, sex is fun! I don't know why I denied myself so long.

Too many barriers up, I guess. I was unwilling to let

anyone see me in a vulnerable position. It's hard to believe that of all the people to let in, I chose Bo Fenton, the guy who hates my guts.

Only maybe he doesn't. Not anymore.

Maybe he never did.

Was this all some crazy, animal attraction that we both resented because we're not supposed to be together?

Me, because I can't. And him because he blames me for what happened to his brother?

He's still watching me, expression almost tender. He reaches out and strums my nipple with the pad of his thumb. "Are you okay?"

I nod.

"Sore?"

"Yeah, a little."

He winces and eases out. "Sorry. I lost control at the end." He turns around and walks to the bathroom, giving me a view of his very nicely-defined butt. I like how unabashed he is about being naked. But with a body like that, who wouldn't be?

I grab his t-shirt from the floor and pull it over my head, not quite so immodest.

When he comes back, he says, "I wrapped the condom up in a bunch of toilet paper. Think it's okay? Who empties the garbage?"

"Oh! Um, I'll make sure to take it out." Oh God, I think I'm blushing.

Bo reaches for me, settling his hands on my waist, stroking the fabric of his t-shirt over my sides. "I like you in my clothes. A lot."

Lord help me, he seems sincere. And that, more than anything, terrifies me.

The cat and dog frenemy thing we had going worked for me. I knew how to play it. But this? This I can't handle.

He wraps a big paw behind my head and pulls my face up to his for another knee-weakening kiss. I want to surrender to it. Want to surrender to him—to just give into whatever the hell this is, whatever the hell he wants.

But it's too dangerous.

My heart can't be in play here.

I need to have enough cash by the time mafia dude gets back, or I'm screwed. And Bo is a distraction, at best. More of a liability. And if we get caught together by the police, they will be quick to draw lines between us. I could end up in jail. Bo could end up with charges against him, and he's done nothing. And Rikki would end up naked in a cage with a ball gag in her mouth.

"Bo." I press my hands against his chest and turn my face away. "It's time for you to leave."

He catches my jaw and turns me back to him. Our foreheads almost touch, but the mood has shifted dramatically. A wire of tension runs through him. He's hyper alert, like he knows exactly what I'm thinking. What I'm up to. "Not happening, sugar."

"You're not solving Winslow's problems sticking around. You hang with me tomorrow, and your life could turn out way worse."

"You're on another job?"

Not much gets by this guy.

I swallow and nod. I have to steal *and* sell a car tomorrow, which means there's no time for getting a title. I'll have to go the most dangerous, stupid route for car thieves. Take it across the border to Mexico and be lucky to get a third of its value.

I have a name and a phone number of a guy to call when I get a car, and he'll give me instructions for the meet up.

My chances of even making it out of the country without getting picked up are slim, but I have to try.

His grip on my jaw tightens. "Why, Sloane? What's the pinch?"

I can't pull away, he's holding me too tightly. I catch his wrist and tap it, pleading for mercy. "Let me go."

His eyes narrow, but after a beat, he releases me and curses. He stalks over and picks up his boxer briefs and steps into them.

"Winslow wouldn't want you to be a part of this. So walk away now, Bo. You've punished me enough. Don't fuck up your own life."

He stands still, staring out the window like he's thinking it over. I try to walk past him to find some shorts to pull on, but he catches me around the waist, pulling my back up against his front.

My breath leaves me in a whoosh.

His arm is like an iron band, but his head rests against mine, like we're slow dancing. "I'll leave in the morning," he murmurs against my ear.

A flush of warm tingles wash over me.

He's staying for me. I mean, for him. Because he wants to be with me.

Not to torture me. Not to find Winslow.

He wants to spend the night.

I want him to spend the night, too.

Especially now that I know he'll leave. I cover his forearm with my hand and squeeze. He nips my ear, and then suddenly, I'm off my feet, up in his arms.

He carries me to the bed and tosses me on it.

The headboard hits the wall, and I put a finger to my lips in warning.

He just grins down at me, his silver eyes glinting dangerously in the lamplight. Beautiful.

"How do you not have a girlfriend?" I blurt. It really seems impossible.

He shrugs. "Because I'm a dick."

I laugh because it's true. He *is* a dick. And also because it's a lie. There's so much more to him than that cocky swagger.

He crawls over me. The dog tag slides across his perfect chest as he moves. "You wanna know what they call me and my friends at school?"

More warmth floods me. He's sharing a piece of himself. It's a moment of normalcy between us. Something we haven't had much of. "What?"

"The alpha-holes. Because we're all walking dicks."

I bring my hands to his thighs, squeeze to feel their hardness. Then I reach up and catch the military tag.

Almost immediately, the air changes. He catches my hand to stop me from looking. We stare at each other.

"Who died?" I ask softly.

He's silent for a moment. There's an air of resentment in his stare, but he finally answers, "My dad."

"I'm sorry."

He releases my hand, lets me turn the tag over and read it.

Theodore Fenton, Navy SEAL.

"How old were you?" I whisper.

"Eight."

He drops beside me, the playfulness gone. But I can't regret this moment. Seeing Bo's wounds exposed.

"Tell me yours," he says after a beat.

My what? I don't ask, though. I know what he means. My wound. My pain. The thing I don't want people to see.

I can't tell him about the mafia, but I can tell him what any asshole who googles me could find out.

"My dad went to jail for embezzlement. That's why I moved here."

Bo leans up on his forearm, his brows drawn together as he studies my face. He brushes a few strands of hair out of my eyes. "Yeah?"

I nod. "We were wealthy. Lived in the best neighborhood. I drove my dad's old Beamer to school. And then wham-o. One day the Feds showed up and raided the house. They arrested my dad and took all but my personal possessions. And I lost everything. He committed suicide in jail six weeks ago."

That's the part I haven't dealt with. Not at all. Not my guilt over not speaking to him after he went to prison. Over not opening the letters he sent before he died. The ones that might have held the information the don is trying to squeeze out of me.

"Fuck, Sloane. That's rough." Bo traces his index finger lightly over my skin, starting at my collarbone and traveling down between my breasts, then around to circling one nipple. "Your mom?"

"Died in childbirth. Me and my dad weren't tight. He was pretty formal and distant, and I think he resented me for my mom's death. But he was what I knew."

"Is your aunt his sister?"

"No, my mom's. So I barely knew her. She's great, though. I should be more grateful to her for taking me in. I just hate —" my voice breaks, and I stop speaking. This is too much.

Bo touches my chin to turn my face back. "Hate what?"

Tears fill my eyes. "I don't know."

"Yes, you do. Tell me."

"I'm just tiptoeing around, afraid any day I'll get kicked out and lose it all again. I mean, what happens when I graduate? There's no money for college. I might get a little scholarship money, but not enough. I don't even know what I'll do." And that's *if* I even live past next month with the mafia situation.

His fingers splay over my belly. "That's why you're stealing cars? For college?"

I blow out a puff of breath. "No."

My answer came too quickly. I should've just let him believe it. It's not a bad story.

"Then why?"

"Enough questions." I try to roll away, but he catches me around the waist and tugs me back.

"Okay."

"Okay?" I'm surprised at his agreement.

"Yeah, I'll back off." He settles on his back with his hands behind his head. I reach over and turn off the lamp.

I want to stay turned away from him, but it feels wrong, so I roll over to face him.

"You still going to do the job tomorrow?"

My stomach squeezes. I have to. The don will be back soon, and I've nothing on his bars of gold and painting. So I'd damn well better have something to give him. To buy my own freedom. "Yeah."

His breath comes out, like he's disappointed. "I don't want to help you," he says into the darkness.

His words hit my solar plexus like a blow. There's resentment in them, and yet I understand the subtext. He doesn't want to, but he does.

"You're not going to help me," I say firmly. "Winslow made me swear not to make you a part of it."

"Then how are you going to sell it?"

"I have a plan." The defensive note to my voice probably clues him into the holes in my plan, but I don't care. I'm not going to ask him to get involved. Although a quick paint job might give the heist a fighting chance of success. No—I'm keeping him out of it.

"You have a plan." His voice drips with disbelief.

"Bo? If you're staying tonight, you're not going to be a dick."

In the darkness, I think I see the corners of his lips kick up. He rolls to bury his face in my neck. "Look at you, laying down the law," he rumbles in my ear. He bites my neck, then kisses it. "Just because I let you ride on top doesn't mean you're calling the shots."

"Tonight I am."

I don't know why I think I can. His threat from last night to turn me in to the cops still stands, but we both know he won't. Just like I wouldn't alert my aunt to his presence. He's going to let me call the shots simply because I'm calling them. Because despite his dickishness, he does respect me.

And maybe because I let him punch my V-card tonight, but I don't want to hang it on that, it's too narrow and cliche.

But yes, because we've been intimate—that's why.

Some of our barriers have come down, and there's a new relationship growing underneath. Friendship, even. And friends respect each other's boundaries.

He kisses my neck again, and I take it as his agreement. With a big hand on my hip, he rolls me to face away from him and molds himself to my back. "Is this spooning?" he murmurs in my ear.

I can't stop the giggle from rising in my throat. "Yep."

"You're my first spoon, Sloane McCormick."

"You're my first ride."

He bites my shoulder. "You liked it."

"I did."

"Any time you wanna ride my cock, it's at your service, princess." Said anatomy twitches at my ass.

"You know just how to ruin a moment, don't you, Fenton?"

He chuckles in my ear and pulls me closer. "It's Fenton now, is it? Yeah, well, I told you I'm a dick. You should've believed it."

"And I told you..." I let the unspoken remainder of the sentence hang in the darkness between us. I don't actually want to kick him out. This is the closest I've felt to another human being in a long time. Maybe ever. And my body's purring with the pleasure he's shown me and still providing.

"You did. Shutting up."

"Thank you." I snuggle back into him, warmth flowing through my limbs.

Tomorrow we'll sever these ties, but just for tonight, I get to enjoy the feeling of being held in a guy's arms. A very hot, very wonderful guy who I can't keep.

CHAPTER 8

o

"HAPPY BIRTHDAY, SLOANE!" two chirpy female voices sing out.

Fuck me!

I roll off the far side of the bed and squeeze under it just as Sloane's bedroom door swings wide.

I'd heard the sound of voices downstairs, and I should've gotten up and dressed and out of here, but I couldn't bring myself to leave Sloane's bed. Not when holding her felt so right.

Not when leaving her meant saying goodbye.

I watch two pairs of feet enter the room and stand inside the door. Then the voices break into a round of "Happy Birthday."

It's sweet, but I fear Sloane's too freaked out about my presence under the bed to appreciate it. I detect the scent of something sweet and chocolatey and the wax of a burning candle.

"Oh my God, you guys. Thank you."

I love the rust in Sloane's voice. It's so damn sexy. She blows and the light scent of smoke reaches my nostrils. One candle, probably. In a cupcake. Or maybe a muffin.

"Happy eighteenth, sweetie," her aunt says. "I know this isn't where you thought you'd spend it, but I want you to know how much we love having you here."

Sloane doesn't answer at first—I'm guessing she's holding back tears. "Thanks," she says.

"Any plans for today?"

"Um… yeah. I'm going to meet up with Bo, my date from last night. We're going to hang out all day. Maybe tonight, too, I'm not sure."

My gut tightens. I'd be satisfied if I thought it was true, but I realize immediately, I'm her cover.

For the job she plans to pull today.

And she's right, I should just walk away and leave her to it. Walk away and never look back.

But I don't like the idea of her pulling this job on her own. I think she's capable as shit, but she's a human. Fragile. If she gets shot by cops, she won't recover.

I just don't like it.

"That's great," her aunt says from above the bed. "Well, maybe tomorrow we can celebrate your birthday together? Go out to dinner or something?"

"Yeah, thanks. That sounds fun."

"Do you want your present now?" Rikki asks.

"Oh, you didn't have to get me a present," Sloane protests.

I'm suddenly pissed as hell I didn't think to get her

one. I knew it was her birthday today—I saw it on her license Thursday. But that seems like a million years ago. Before an ocean of change washed between us.

Before I knew what her pain consisted of.

Loss, but also unworthiness. She feels like an outsider—doesn't think she belongs here in this townhouse, with these people. Sounds like she never belonged with her dad, either.

And all I've done is grind in that sentiment a little deeper.

Regret washes through me. No wonder she let me push her around—feeling blameworthy resonates for her.

"We got you a present," Rikki tells her. "Should we save it for dinner tomorrow?"

"Yeah, let's save it for the celebration," Sloane says. The bed shifts as she climbs out of it. "I can't wait." Her bare feet move toward the bathroom. "I'm going to jump in the shower. Thank you for my birthday muffin." She's trying to get them out of the room. Clever girl.

"All right, sweetie. There are more muffins downstairs if you want. Rikki made a whole batch."

"Thank you, Rikki. It's delicious."

Her bedroom door shuts, and Sloane rushes over to the side of the bed where I'm sitting up.

"Oh my God." She covers her mouth with her hand and drops to her knees in front of me, stifling giggles. "I can't believe you rolled off the bed so fast!"

"Good thing they didn't hear the thud of my body hitting the floor." I grab her and pull her into my lap, dropping a kiss on her temple. "Happy birthday, princess."

"Ugh." Clearly this birthday is a trigger for all that's wrong in her life.

Dammit.

I want to fix it for her. All of it.

And that's impossible because I'm leaving today.

All I can do is help her forget. I lift her out of my lap and stand up, then scoop her up into my arms.

"What are you doing?" She kicks her legs.

"Taking you to the shower. Isn't that where you were going?" I carry her to the bathroom and silently turn the locks on both doors before I lower her to her feet.

I turn on the water.

She stands there with her arms folded across her chest, looking adorable in my t-shirt and her rumpled hair.

I hold my hand out. "Do you trust me?"

A reluctant smile curls her lips. "Yeah. I don't know why, but I do." She puts her hand in mine. I tug my t-shirt off over her head, then drop the boxer briefs to the floor and lead her into the tub.

I pick up the bar of soap and roll it in one hand, gathering lather. "All right birthday girl. Tell me how you want to come."

She watches the soap. "Do you have another condom?"

I lift my brows. "You want to come on my cock?"

"Maybe."

I grip the base of said cock and give it a hard yank. "Don't tease it. I'm fully prepared to go blue-balled for you again if you tell me you want the vibrator. Or my mouth. Or fingers. It's *your* birthday, princess."

I love the slow smile that spreads across her face. "That's very gallant of you." She jerks her head toward her bedroom. "Go get a condom."

"Don't have to tell me twice," I mutter, heading to the bedroom. I grab a condom from my wallet and quickly return.

When I get back, her nipples are hard peaks, and her fingers are between her legs.

"Oh, sugar." This girl will be the death of me. I thought I worked through the crazy hormones of puberty, but I'm ready to jizz before we've even started.

But it's her birthday, and then I'm gone, so I have to make it good.

I pick up the bar of soap again and lather it up, then stroke down her neck, across her shoulder, around her breast.

She trails one finger down my abs, and my cock punches out even harder. I stroke her other breast and down her belly. Then I drop to my knees and trail my hands down her thighs.

I look up, through water droplets on my lids to watch her face when I scoop behind one knee to pull it over my shoulder.

And then I give it to her—full bore. I suck and lick and nip. I taste her like I'm a starving man. She grips my shoulders, pulls my hair, wobbles on her standing leg.

"I won't let you fall," I promise, wrapping one arm around her waist and palming her ass with the other.

"I want you inside me," she says.

I grin, my knees cracking as I stand up. "I love a girl who knows what she wants."

"Also, I don't want to run out of hot water before we're done." Her smile lights up my entire world.

I snap open the condom wrapper and roll on protection. "You want it from behind?"

She hesitates. Well, duh. How would she know how she wants it? Last night was her first time.

I take her hips and turn her around, guiding her hands to the wall, then shift the shower head, so it's not dumping water in her face. "It's easier for standing. But if you want to watch my muscles, I'll gladly hold you up and fuck you senseless against the other wall."

She tosses her wet hair over her shoulder and gives me a smoldering look. "This way. But still senseless."

I rub the head of my cock in her juices. "Your wish is my command."

She pants a little as I enter her. "Still sore?"

"A little. But it's good. Keep going."

Damn. I have to remember how slowly humans heal. I was way too rough with her last night.

Not that she didn't take it beautifully.

I press in, inch by inch, until I'm seated. I shudder at how incredible it feels, my breath turning ragged. But this is about her. I can't lose control. I grasp her wet hips and pump, slowly at first. When she starts moaning, I pick up speed. My vision sharpens and domes, like when I'm in wolf form, which hasn't happened during sex before. It's almost like my wolf thinks she's my mate. I'm fucking on fire for this girl.

When *I* start moaning—not really, but I want to—I reach around and rub her clit.

She goes off immediately—faster than I expected, her tight cunt gripping and releasing my cock in quick squeezes.

I don't last even a second longer. I clamp my mouth tight around a full-wolf snarl as I slam in hard, my loins slapping loudly against her wet ass, my fingers digging into her flesh. Three thrusts. Four. Five.

And then I shoot my load, filling the condom as stars dance in front of my eyes from the heat and pleasure.

When I can speak again—when I can move—I wrap my arms around her from behind, my cock still filling her. "Happy birthday, princess," I murmur in her ear.

She looks over her shoulder at me. Her gaze is soft. "Thanks. It's definitely a memorable one."

I kiss her shoulder, then ease out. "Don't forget to take out the trash in here, yeah?" I step out of the shower to dispose of the condom the same way I did the last one.

"I won't."

I'm not into goodbyes. I suck at them, actually, so I'm suddenly itchy to get out of here. I'm actually itchy to run. Like, in wolf form.

Like there's something emerging in me that needs to get worked out.

She turns off the water, and I hand her a towel. "I'm going to jet."

She nods. She still wants to get rid of me. This is how it's supposed to go down.

"If you run into trouble today, call me. I'll be there. That's a promise."

She cocks her head. "Why?" Her voice is soft and scratchy.

"Fuck if I know, Legs. Because you're you. And I'm not pissed anymore."

She nods, stepping out of the tub with those long, muscular legs that rock my world so hard. She's every guy's wet dream right now, with the towel not quite closed in front, her perfect tits and glimpses of her pussy showing through.

"Thanks."

I stand there, staring. I want to kiss her, but it doesn't feel right. Like we're standing on two icebergs that have already separated and are drifting apart.

"I mean it about calling me. I don't *want* to help you, but I definitely will. Okay?"

"Bye, Bo."

My chest hurts for some reason. "Bye. Be careful, Legs. Don't get caught."

I pull on my boxer briefs and t-shirt, then go to her bedroom and put on a pair of jeans, stuffing the rest of my shit into my backpack.

I open the window before she comes out of the bathroom. The sooner I get out of here, the better, considering my chances of being seen are sky high. Still, I hesitate, looking around. I want to give her something, to leave something, but I have nothing to offer. Not even a card for her goddamn birthday.

I scratch a quick note on the pad on her desk. Just the same thing I told her in the bathroom. *If you need help, I'll be there.*

Look at me, offering to be her knight in shining armor.

I can't help myself. My wolf's already whining about leaving her in danger. He doesn't seem to care she's a human and a pain in my ass.

He just wants her to be safe.

Fuck.

I slip out the window and throw myself to the side to drop all the way to the ground below.

It's way past time for me to be gone.

CHAPTER 9

loane

I CAN'T SHAKE off the bubble of warmth Bo left me with. I'm trawling the Scottsdale streets on my bike, looking for a luxury car to steal, but my mind is still back in my bedroom.

Still back at the dance, seeing Bo grinning through bloody teeth, like he loved getting his ass kicked.

Crazy heroic baller.

God, I'm falling for him hard.

But the falling stops now. Today. Because I'm not seeing him again, and it's over.

And I need to bring laser focus to this operation, or I will be in deep shit. Deeper shit than I already am.

It takes me several hours of riding my bike around, but eventually I stumble on the perfect car.

Well, the perfect, most horrible car.

It's an orange corvette. Racing style. I'm pretty sure some drug dealer in Mexico will freaking love it.

The hard part will be keeping a low profile with this baby while I get there.

Did I say hard? I meant impossible.

But whatever. I knew the chances of success for today's job were far lower than usual.

I do my thing and am gone in sixty seconds.

Actually, it was more like two minutes, but yeah, I have that sixty second thing in my mind every time I steal a car.

I get on I-10 and beeline it for Tucson, making the call to my contact, Jorge, on the way.

"What do you have?" he demands.

"2017 Corvette Z06, perfect condition. You want it? If not, I have another buyer."

"I want it," he says. "How soon can you bring it?"

"How much are you paying?"

He mutters something in Spanish, then says, "I can do ten, maybe fifteen grand, depends on the condition."

Dammit. That's half of what I could get if I could get a clean title. But I knew that would be the case.

"Fifteen or I'm not coming down."

"No, it depends on the condition. I'm not gonna make an offer until I see it. Bring it down here, and we'll discuss."

I blow out my breath. "Fine. I'll be there by tonight. I can get it to the border, but I don't know how to get it across."

"I'll worry about that. Come to Naco. I'll text you an address."

"Naco? Is that near Nogales?"

He makes a scoffing sound. "No, different crossing. Google-map that shit. Text me when you're there."

"Yep," I say to a dead phone because he already hung up.

I try to shove down the mounting sense of dread I have about this transaction. *It will be all right. It will be all right. I can totally do this.*

Bo

I WORK my ass off at the body shop, trying to finish up Winslow's open jobs while fielding the third degree from my uncle, but all the time, I have this nagging feeling I need to get back to Cave Hills.

Make sure everything went straight for Sloane.

I really fucking hate the idea of her trying to fence a car on her own. It means she'd be dealing with dirtbags and considering the way she looks? She could be in the worst kind of danger there is.

And I'd fucking kill any thug who hurt her.

I pull out my phone to check to see if she's texted.

She hasn't.

I wonder where she is right now. What has her in such a bind that she needs to spend her birthday risking her freedom and her life for a heist.

And then I remember that tracking app I put on her phone. Did she notice? My thumb flies over my screen to pull it up, and then I hit the dot with her name on it.

There she is.

Fuck!

She's on the highway, headed to Tucson.

I don't like it.

I really don't fucking like it.

I wipe my hands on a rag. "Hey, Uncle Greg. I gotta go."

"What? Is it about Winslow?"

"Maybe. Yeah. I'm gonna find out. I'll try to come in tomorrow, okay?"

My uncle swears, but he's shaking his head, like he's already written my help off. "Just stay out of trouble, Bo."

"Yep. I will."

That's probably a lie.

I get on my bike because Winslow's car would attract too much attention. Besides, I can go faster on the Triumph —weave between traffic if I need to.

I don't know why getting to Sloane feels like such a goddamn emergency, but it does. I kick the bike to life and take off, not even taking the time to text my mom. I'll let her know when I get there.

I ride fast, the wind rushing past me satisfying that need I had to let my wolf out to run.

Yes. Drive fast. Get to Sloane, he whispers.

And I obey. She didn't ask for my help, but it looks like she's getting it, whether she wants it or not.

~

SLOANE

. . .

NACO, Arizona is a tiny border town past Sierra Vista. I get there before sunset and text Jorge.

He doesn't answer right away, which makes me nervous as hell. I am so out of my element here, it's not even funny. I end up parking behind a school and scrunching down in the seat to browse my Instagram.

It's full of photos from Homecoming—Cave Hills kids looking glamorous as they play dress up. I'm tagged in a bunch.

There's one of Bo and I that makes my heart double-pump. We're on the dance floor and his arm is around my back. He's smiling down at me with this indulgent sort of amusement.

Because that's when we were playing games.

I was horning him up rubbing my body all over his. Clearly, he was enjoying it but had himself under control.

I'm not sure I've ever met a guy like him. He's so damn cocky, and yet that confidence is completely deserved. He does have it all—good looks, athletic talent, charm. He's definitely the alpha-hole they call him at his school—in charge and at large.

The buzz of a motorcycle nearby makes me sink lower in my seat, even though the windows are tinted. I'm definitely not blending in with this orange hot rod.

A tap at my window makes me scream, and then my heart somersaults.

Bo.

I roll down the window. "What are you doing here?"

"I followed you," he says.

"Why?" I push open the door and climb out, my body stiff from the long drive.

"I told you—white on rice."

"You told me glue. And I told you to stay out of this. Bo, you definitely don't want to be here for this."

He shrugs. He's back to surly Bo, looking kind of pissed off to be here, but maybe that's because he rode a motorcycle for four hours to follow me.

Not my fault.

"I'm here. What's the plan?"

Despite my protest, I'm beyond relieved to have Bo with me. I was scared shitless about what comes next.

"I'm waiting for a text telling me where to bring it."

"Okay. So we wait. You hungry?"

"Starved," I admit.

"Me too." He glances at the car. "That's a pretty sweet fucking ride."

I can't help but grin. "It really is. Wanna drive it?"

He's a car guy. He grew up in a body shop. He works on them for a living. I can tell he appreciates the hell out of this Corvette. He wants to sit behind the wheel. But he says the right thing: "Nah."

I shouldn't push. But he's already becoming my accomplice. So he might as well get the pleasure of at least driving the stolen car. "Zero to sixty in 2.95 seconds. Get in. I know you want to drive her."

I walk around to the passenger's side and climb in.

Bo lets out a low curse and drops down into the driver's seat, scooting it even farther back than I had it. He fastens his seatbelt and shuts the door.

"Fuck, yeah, I want to drive her."

He takes off, peeling out of the parking lot and racing down the back roads. "Get on Google maps and find me a deserted road where I can tear around."

I do, and I tell him how to get there.

He stops the car and revs the engine. "You gonna clock her?"

I open the timer function on my phone and nod. "Ready in 3...2...1!"

He takes off, the tires screaming. The car shoots to sixty, then seventy, then eighty and ninety. "Hang on, Legs!" he shouts and hits the brakes to make a tight turn.

I scream with exhilaration, and Bo laughs like a maniac as he gets it back up to ninety going the other direction.

Back and forth he tests the car, making me clutch the door handle with white knuckles while thrills of excitement drench my body.

After about twenty minutes, my voice is hoarse from screaming, and my neck's starting to hurt from trying to hold my head on for the tight turns.

Bo flips one more turn and heads back toward Naco. "Nope, we can't sell it. I'm keeping this baby."

"Right? I don't think anyone would notice. It's not like it's flashy or anything."

"No kidding. You couldn't pick another boring Mercedes sedan or something? You had to go for the race car?"

I shrug. "Desperate times."

He sobers, giving me a long look as we pull up to a stop sign. "Are they, Legs?"

My chest cinches up, and I refuse to look his way. "Weren't you going to get some food?"

"Yep. I'm going to the Burger King drive-thru. I saw it on the way in."

I didn't. I narrow my eyes. "How did you follow me, exactly?"

"App on your phone. Thanks, by the way—for not shutting off your location services."

"Yeah, I needed them to find this little town. I didn't know my stalker had made my phone a tracking device."

"I came to save your ass, so a little less attitude and a whole lot more gratitude is in order, sugar."

"I don't recall asking you to be my savior." Although the truth is, I'm steeped in gratitude right now. When he knocked on my window, I'd never been so happy to see a friendly face in my life.

Especially his.

He pulls into the Burger King parking lot and orders four burgers and three french fries. Then he looks at me. "What are you having?"

I smack him with the back of my hand. "Are you serious?"

He grins at me and turns back to the speaker. "And a Sprite. That's it." As he pulls forward, he says, "I hope you have money."

I snort and pull out my wallet. "What would you do if I didn't?"

"Zero to sixty in 2.95 seconds."

I laugh.

We pick up the food, and Bo tears into a burger with one hand while he drives. It's gone in 2.95 seconds.

"Holy shit, you probably could eat all four of these yourself," I marvel, unwrapping another burger to hand to him.

My phone beeps with a text, and I grab it, my mood shifting to tension. "I have the address."

"All right, let's go." Bo's voice rings with a can-do timbre. It's damn sexy on him.

He drives to the parking lot where he first showed up and gets out. "I'll follow on my bike."

I walk around to climb in the driver's side. "You don't have to."

He shakes his head. "No fucking way I'm letting you go to that meet without backup. I'm your goddamn muscle."

I fall into him, squeezing both his biceps as I incline my head against his chest. "You're a prince, Bo."

"I thought I was the knight." He palms the back of my neck. "And you're the queen. Let's move."

CHAPTER 10

o

THE HAIRS on the back of my neck prickle with danger from the moment we arrive at the meet location.

Naco is sketchy to begin with, and this abandoned lot is even worse. Darkness has fallen, and there are no street-lights—not that I need them, but the fact that these guys picked a dark abandoned lot doesn't bode well.

Of course, they don't want to get caught by the cops, either.

I just have a feeling Sloane's going to get screwed on this deal.

I leave my motorcycle behind a concrete hut of some kind. I can't tell what this place used to be. Then I walk around and get in the passenger side of Sloane's car.

"You have a gun?"

She jerks like I shot her. "Fuck, no. You think we need one?"

I shrug. It's not like I know how to use one, anyway. But it might be good to wave around and threaten assholes with. But seeing her anxiety ramp up, I wish I hadn't said it. "Nah, I think we're fine. I could probably take three guys, maybe four."

I'm speaking realistically, but Sloane frowns. "You couldn't take the three guys at the dance."

Right. Shit.

Because I'm trying to calm her, not freak her out more, I opt for the truth. "Honestly, Legs? I was holding back. My coach would've killed me if I got in trouble for fighting at another school's dance. I mean seriously kicked my ass down the field and back."

She stares at me. I hear the thud of her heart, and I wonder if I said too much. If she realizes there's something different about me.

"So that's why you were smiling," she says incredulously. "You really didn't care at all about getting hit."

I catch her arm, my sensitive hearing picking up the sound of car tires on gravel. "They're coming."

We both climb out of the corvette. I shake out my limbs, like I'm getting ready for a big game.

Or a fight.

Three guys climb out of a white Cadillac Escalade, and I swear to fate, I smell menace on them. They circle the Corvette, admiring her.

As they should.

"Which one of you is Jorge?" Sloane asks. The girl is a pro at not allowing her fear to bleed through her tone or body language. She doesn't look like a high school student who is way out of her depths.

She's a badass criminal, who looks hot as hell while she's breaking laws and skulls.

"I am." Jorge has the driver side door open and is looking in at the ignition. "Where are the keys?"

"You'll get the keys when I get the money."

He shakes his head. "No can do. I need to make sure she runs."

"She runs. Are we making a deal or not?"

Jorge strolls over to Sloane, casual-like, but I don't trust him for a minute. I step closer, looming behind her, my arms folded across my chest like a personal bodyguard.

I'm watching his hands. They are casual, by his sides. "The keys, bitch. Give them to me. Now."

His fingers curl, but I'm too late to stop it. He punches her in the gut.

My fist connects with his temple, and he goes down hard.

He comes up with a gun pointed in the center of my chest.

"No!" Sloane screams and the crazy girl tries to jump in front of me.

I shove her—way too hard because I'm already shifting. The sound of her body hitting the pavement makes me snarl in fury. One bullet hits my side.

My teeth snap. Another bullet catches my hip. My clothes rip, and I'm on the shooter in a single leap. The gun gets knocked away, but I miss his throat, biting a chunk of his shoulder instead. His arms come up in protection, and we wrestle, me trying to finish the fucker.

There are shouts behind me. Sloane screams *No!* at the top of her lungs.

I whirl to see one of the guys bending over her, and I leave my prey, growling and snarling, ready to pounce.

I'm too late, though. The guy leaps through the open door of the Corvette and starts it up. He's driving it away before the door's even shut.

The Escalade peels out, too, stopping to drag the guy I mauled into the vehicle.

And then they're both gone.

They're gone, and Sloane's retching on the pavement.

And she just saw my wolf.

Fuck.

~

SLOANE

BO IS A WOLF. As fucked up and crazy as that sounds, I can't be wrong. The clothes he was wearing are tangled around the giant wolf's body. And there's no mistaking his father's dog tag hanging from the chain around its neck.

Even knowing it's Bo, I crab walk backward on the pavement when it comes near me.

It's scary as hell—way bigger than a normal wolf, it's teeth dripping with blood, silver eyes narrowed with fury. It's fur is silver, too, only bloodstained from the gunshot wounds.

There's a blur of motion, a crunch and cracking of bones, and then Bo's crouching over me, his ripped clothes hanging off him.

"Fuck, Sloane," he curses. His eyes still glow silver with rage. He scoops me into his arms and runs for the bike. He sits me on the seat, then opens the saddlebag and produces a pair of jeans. I guess when you can spontaneously turn into a wolf, you have to keep extra pants around for moments like these.

He kicks off the ruined jeans and shoves his legs into the new pair. His phone, socks and sneakers are on the pavement where they fell off. He grabs them and barely has his feet shoved in his shoes when we hear sirens.

"Son of a bitch." He shoves the helmet my way, then kickstarts the motorcycle and roars around the concrete building, driving through overgrown weeds and brush until we bump over curbs and emerge on a back street.

I cling to his torn t-shirt, which is barely hanging on. I bunch a handful of it together to staunch the wound on his side.

But clearly, it's not bothering him.

Because he's not a fucking human!

My mind whips back to every interaction we've had. Any clues I should've caught about this, this… guy? Wolf? Whatever the hell he is.

Well, duh. He's from *Wolf Ridge.*

Holy shit—are all the people there werewolves? Was Winslow? That's why Bo didn't think he was dead after getting shot by the cops?

And the fight at school. That's why he was just laughing when he got beat up. And how he never sported a bruise or any sign of it after he brushed his teeth of the blood.

It's why Wolf Ridge wins all the sporting events.

Why his eyes seemed to change color. They *were* changing—to the color of his wolf's eyes!

I should be more freaked out than I am. My mind is still reeling, but my body? My body's one hundred percent on board. Bo is a wolf. A bonafide, howls at the moon, shapeshifting wolf.

My nipples peak and thighs tighten around his hips. No wonder he's literally an animal in bed.

No wonder his body is a work of art. His muscles unbelievably big. His movements so agile.

And right now, he's all business.

He doesn't stop to talk or make a plan, he just zips through the back streets of Naco until he gets on the state highway, then I-10.

I don't complain.

My belly aches from getting punched, and my side is one giant road rash from Bo pushing me out of the way of the bullet.

None of that matters, though.

What matters is that I don't have any money to give the don's men tomorrow. Which means my life is over.

For a moment, I consider involving Bo. Could he fight them off for me? Kill them?

But no, the don is too powerful for one high school kid to take on—even if he is superhuman. These guys were just associates of his. If they disappear, he'll send more. Serious ones, from Detroit. Not these Arizona idiots he hired.

And they won't stop coming. Not until the don gets his pound of flesh.

Besides, I don't know if it's true that bullets can't hurt Bo. Maybe he's dying right now and just has a really high pain threshold. I lift the shirt away from the wound I was staunching, but I don't feel blood gushing beneath it.

I bring my fingertip to the wound, touching as lightly as possible. He doesn't wince. I probe it a little more. Feel the bullet lodged near the surface.

I work it out with my fingertips, half-shocked, half-satisfied when it pops out into my palm.

"Thanks," Bo shouts over the wind.

It's the first thing he's said since we left.

Remembering where the second wound is beneath his jeans, I work my fingers down past his waistband until I find it and work the second bullet out.

Okay, yeah. Definitely superhuman strength and healing abilities.

"Sloane—are you okay?" he shouts.

"I'm okay." I mean, I'm in pain, but big picture, fine. No bullet wounds. No broken bones.

There's so much more I want to say, but it's impossible with the wind and the speed. And besides, I still sense anger and tension radiating from him.

I don't know if it's just leftover aggression or if he's mad at me. Either way, I'm not going to poke the bear. I mean, wolf.

Fall is still warm in Arizona, but I get cold on the ride with the sun down and the wind whipping at us. I'm beyond grateful when Bo takes one of the Tucson exits—I don't think I could stand another two plus hours back home.

CHAPTER 11

loane

Bo drives downtown and parks beside a row of motorcycles in a lot behind what looks like a nightclub. The city is hopping. Young people pack the back patio and music thumps from inside.

We both dismount from the bike, and I pull off the helmet.

Bo crowds into me, his eyes still glinting silver, his form still tense and angry. He wraps a fist in my hair in the back and brings his face right up to mine. "You'll take it to the grave with you," he growls.

I suddenly understand his tension. I saw something I wasn't supposed to see.

"What you saw back there. You won't speak a word of it to anyone. *Ever.* Understand?"

Menacing Bo is frightening, but it turns me on.

Knowing the cocky roguish flirt—the guy with all that easy-going charm—turns into a two hundred pound deadly weapon when threatened ignites some primitive part of my brain. Male as protector. Or provider. Or general bad-ass you want on your side.

"I won't. I promise."

"Swear it." I hear the growl of the wolf in his voice.

"I swear."

He looks at me a moment longer, then releases my hair. "I'm gonna ask for help here. Don't speak unless you're spoken to, or you're damn sure I want you to. Got it?"

Got it. Bo is in charge.

I can roll with that.

I can definitely roll with it.

He turns and stalks toward the back entrance of the club. I have to hurry to catch up with his long strides.

"No entrance here," the bouncer growls as we walk up. "Go around front to get I.D.s checked."

I.D.s. Shit.

"We're not coming in. I just need to talk to a manager. Is Jared here? Or Tank?"

The bouncer looks at him closer, taking in the torn, bloody shirt and blood-stained jeans. He leans forward a little and sniffs.

Okay. Another wolf, then.

I look at the sign over the back of the club. Eclipse. A moon reference. So this is a werewolf club.

He touches a comm unit in his ear. "Jared, I need you at the back gate."

A huge tattooed guy appears from the building, his attention trained on us. He examines Bo as he walks up. "Fenton. Winslow's brother, right?"

"Yeah, Bo." He holds out his hand, and the two shake.

"I'm sorry, man, but you're like, what? Seventeen? I can't let you—" His nostrils flare and his gaze drops to the blood on Bo's shirt. "Fuck. Are you in trouble?"

"Yeah. Is there some place we can stay the night while I heal?"

Jared swears again. "Yeah." He opens the gate and walks out. "You have a ride?"

"I have my bike."

"Good. Follow me."

We walk back to the row of parked motorcycles, and Jared climbs on one. I pull the helmet back on and climb behind Bo.

It's a short ride—less than a mile—and we pull up at a tall downtown apartment building. Jared lets us in, and we ride an elevator up to the fifth floor. When we get there, he unlocks an apartment. It's furnished, but there's nothing personal in it. "This one is empty. There's no food in the fridge, but you can order in."

"Thanks, man. Hey, can you do me one more favor?"

Jared's eyes narrow. "What's that?"

"Don't tell the mayor yet?"

His eyes slide to me, like he's trying to figure out if I know what they are. "I don't work for the mayor. But my, uh, boss, definitely needs to know what's going on. You need to talk to him— tomorrow morning. Don't fucking leave before you do. Understand? Do I have your word?"

Bo swallows and nods. "Yeah."

"All right. You need anything else?" His eyes travel to me again, and his nostrils flare like he's sniffing me. "She hurt?"

"Yeah, she's hurt. I'm gonna take care of her."

"With what, my man? Hang on." He leaves the apartment and comes back a few minutes later with a med kit. "Here. This should have the basics in it."

"Thanks, Jared. I really appreciate it." Bo offers his hand again, only this time they clasp forearms.

"Glad to help. I gotta get back to the club, but I'll see you in the morning." He releases Bo's arm and points a finger in his face. "Seriously, man. If you bail before talking to Garrett, you are toast. Understand me?"

"I won't bail."

"Give me your phone." Jared takes his phone and sends himself a text, judging by the resulting chime from the phone in his pocket. "'Kay. You got me now, too."

"Thanks again."

When Jared leaves, some of the tension drops out of Bo's shoulders, but his face is still a tight mask.

"Sit." He points to a chair in the kitchen.

Again, I'm more turned on than mad that he's so curt. I sit in the chair, and he sets the med kit on the table and opens it, scanning the items like he's never seen them before.

Ha. He probably hasn't.

"Just some ibuprofen would be great." I snag a packet out of the box.

He opens the refrigerator and produces a can of Sprite, which he cracks open and hands to me. "I smell blood."

"It's probably yours."

He pulls my shirt over my head and curses when he sees my shoulder and arm. I wince a little, too, because it's one big raspberry.

"Fuck, Sloane." He slams his fist down on the table, making the med kit pop into the air. "I did this to you."

My heart pounds from the aggression, but I answer him with snark. "You took two bullets for me, Bo. We're good."

He rifles through the kit and produces alcohol wipes.

"I'll do it." I try to grab them out of his hand, but he holds them out of my reach.

"I'm fucking doing it." He rips it open and dabs at my road rash with total concentration.

"Jesus, Bo. Why are you mad?"

A muscle jumps in his jaw. "I'm not *mad*. I'm…"

It hits me then that this might be Bo scared. It's full warrior mode, ready to slay our foes if they return. But maybe he's just ready to slay me for getting him into this.

"You could've died back there," he splutters. "And don't ever try to take a bullet for me again—that was so fucking stupid!"

He must see the shock on my face because he shakes his head and takes a step back. "I'm sorry, I don't mean you're stupid. But you scared the hell out of me. And...I'm in deep shit now. I just violated two pack rules and maybe killed a man. My mom might lose both her sons over your fucking car heists."

I want to yell back that I didn't ask him to come with me, but I can't get the words out. Blood rushes to my face and tears pop into my eyes. Jesus. I held it together this whole semester at school, fooling the entire student body, but with Bo, I show everything.

As soon as he sees them, he turns away and punches a nearby wall. *"Fuck!"*

"I'm sorry," I manage to say through the tears in my throat.

"No." He turns. "No, no, no. I'm the asshole. I'm

sorry." He scrubs a hand over his face. "I can't get back in control. Are my eyes still silver?"

"Yeah, a little." They are half-blue, half silver.

"The kill instinct...it was so fucking strong. I would've killed all of them." He draws a measured breath in through his nostrils and holds it for a moment before he lets it go. "That was my first time experiencing it."

I blink at him. I want to ask a million questions, but I know he's not in the mood. Instead, I offer up my vulnerability. The truth. "I'm really turned on by you right now."

His eyes flash pure pale silver again, and a low growl comes out of his throat.

"Oh, sugar. You don't want to tell me that when I'm in this state. I will fuck you six ways to Sunday. And it won't be respectful."

My pussy clenches with excitement. We lock gazes. I slowly slide off the chair and drop to my knees in front of him.

He groans and squeezes his cock through his jeans. "You're making a mistake," he warns, but he's already unbuttoning. Already freeing his impressive length.

Already hard for me.

Bo

HOLY FUCK. This is not what I should be doing right now.

Not when my wolf is still so close to the surface. Not when aggression still pours from me. Not when I need answers from Sloane about what in the hell she's into that would make her resort to trying to complete such an insanely stupid job.

But she's gripping my cock, opening that gorgeous mouth of hers to take me in. No fucking way I can stop now.

I'm in the throes of ecstasy from the moment her wet tongue touches the head of my cock. I shudder, my balls drawing up tight, my thighs starting to quake. She lifts her gaze to my face and holds it as she swirls her tongue around.

I can't take the tease. I'm way too far gone from that. I grasp the back of her head and shove her over my cock. She gags a little, but it feels too good to let up.

Fuck. I warned her. I wrap my fist in her hair and use it to control her movements, pushing her over my cock and back off, already close to climax.

The room spins. My breath rasps in and out harshly. A sheen of sweat coats my skin. My canines descend, a sweet taste filling my mouth. *Holy shit! My wolf wants to mark her!*

It's crazy. The mating instinct is only supposed to come once in a lifetime, with the she-wolf you're meant to spend the rest of your life with. Sloane isn't even a wolf. But I can't deny the connection I've had with her from the beginning. Even when I hated her shit and wanted her out of the shop and our lives, I still was drawn to her like a magnet.

I suck in measured breaths, trying to shove my wolf back down. I can't mark her—that's insane. But her mouth feels so hot. So delicious. I'm ready to blow.

And I don't want to come in her mouth. I want everything tonight. No—I need it.

Because she's the reason I'm here. The reason I lost

control to save her. The reason I fucked up my whole life. And in this moment, it feels like fucking her hard would make it all worth it.

With great effort, I manage to release my hold on her hair and pull out.

"Up," I command, my voice hoarse and guttural.

I grip her elbow to help her stand.

I'm already consumed in the flames of desire. It's hard to even speak. "Clothes off."

I see my own heat reflected in her gaze as she walks backward, leading me toward the bedroom as she reaches behind her back and unhooks her bra.

A low growl fills the room, and I realize it's coming from me. I quickly close the distance between us and catch her around the waist, using my shifter strength to toss her easily on the bed.

She unbuttons her pants, and I help her out of them, throwing them over my shoulder before ripping off her panties.

I dive between her legs and feast on her juicy pussy. I'm on full throttle. This isn't foreplay, it's a full press home, and I have her first orgasm within sixty seconds. I don't stop.

I flip her over and pull her up to hands and knees, and then I spank her—probably too hard. I slap right cheek then left while she gasps and squirms. I keep it up until my handprints turn her ass a pretty pink, then I spread her cheeks and lick a long line from her slit to her anus and back. I slap her ass a few more times.

"Ouch, Bo. What is that for?" She's breathless, her voice slightly strangled.

"That's your punishment, sugar."

"For what?"

"For making me fall for you." I slap her ass again even though I know she's had enough. "For being so fucking gorgeous." Another slap. "And smart. And fascinating." I rub her blushing cheeks. "For captivating me."

And making me want to mark you, when you're human.

"I didn't want to fall for you, either."

Shit. Is she choking up?

My wolf stills, aggression immediately tamped down. I tackle her down to the bed, turning her over to kiss the hell out of her. Her soft body writhes beneath mine. Our lips twist, tongues lash. When I come up for air, her lips are swollen, eyes glassy.

I cage her throat loosely. "I'm gonna fuck the hell out of you, and then you're gonna tell me everything."

She stops breathing, some of the focus coming back to her eyes. The knot of worry between her brows appearing.

"You have my secrets," I remind her. "You fucking owe me yours."

I don't wait for her agreement. I pull out a condom and roll it on. Then I hesitate, my brain trying to rein in the wolf aggression. Trying to make sure I haven't misread cues.

"Clothes off," she says, mimicking my earlier order.

Yes. Satisfaction punches through me. She does want this.

I grin, yanking off my shirt and shucking the jeans, torn boxer briefs and socks. "Now you're really in trouble." I crawl back over her.

"Bring it, wolf boy."

I rub the head of my cock over her wet slit and push a

little. She's still tight as hell. Knowing I'm the only guy she's allowed between her legs does something to me.

I lose my senses again and thrust hard, filling her completely. She gasps and grasps my arms.

Giving my head a shake, I force myself to hold still. "You okay? "

She arches beneath me. "I said bring it."

With a growl, I surge inside her, rocking in and out, losing my mind even more with each thrust.

She receives me, watching with a lidded gaze, her body rocking to meet mine. When she hooks her ankles around my back, I nearly come, but I roar instead and slam harder.

And then I'm lost. I want it to go on forever, but it's too late. Lightning strikes at the base of my spine and my balls draw up tight.

I come. Hard. So hard my vision turns black and spotty and my canines lengthen like my wolf wants to mark her. Which is just nuts because she's a human.

I turn my face away and keep my upper body lifted and fuck her with short deep thrusts until I finish.

Shit—I've forgotten her pleasure. I bring my thumb to her clit and rub and—thank fuck—she goes off immediately, her pussy clenching around my cock, drawing another release from me.

I wait until my vision clears to drop down and kiss her and come a little more.

"Sloane," I rasp. I don't have anything to say. I'm just uttering her name like an invocation. A celebration.

I kiss her some more, moving slowly inside her, rocking out the last of my climax as she shudders and goes limp beneath me.

I don't ever want to stop kissing and fucking her. I could keep this up all night, but we have shit to discuss.

Huge fucking problems.

So I force myself back and ease out, getting up to dispose of the condom in the bathroom.

There's one thing I will say about all this trouble—it's pretty fucking awesome to have our own private place to stay for the night.

Of course, my mom and her aunt might have a lot to say about it, if they knew.

When I walk back in the bedroom, I pull my phone out of my jeans and text my mom: *I'm in Tucson with Garrett's pack for the night. Still working on finding Winslow. Love you.*

She texts back: *Stop looking for him. I need you at home.*

I groan and stab my fingers through my hair. *Be home tomorrow. Sorry, Mom.*

Mom: *I love you, Bo. Be safe. Text me when you leave Tucson.*

I give her the thumbs up and climb onto the bed where Sloane is still sprawled like a limp doll.

I crawl over her and weave my fingers into her hair. "Was I too rough?"

She blinks at me. "You're always too rough, but now I know why. And I think it's pretty hot."

I'm not prepared for the sensations her words produce. First of all, I'm not used to that soft, intimate voice she's using with me. Nor am I used to the way she watches me, her face open and trusting. But hearing the lust in her voice, her approval of my wolf makes him stand up and preen.

But she's not supposed to know about me. It's pack law. Violations require remedies like having her mind wiped by a leech. Which I know they have plenty of in Tucson. Garrett, the Tucson pack leader and our alpha's son has a tenuous alliance with them, but I know the wolves don't like how many vampires have moved in.

I sit back on my haunches and scrub my hand over my five o'clock shadow. Or in this case, I guess it's a midnight shadow.

"I have your word about the wolf thing," I remind her.

"To the grave," she answers.

"I'm not going to answer questions about it. The less you know, the better. Understand?"

She doesn't like that, I can tell from the little puff of disappointment that comes from her, but she nods.

"Now you spill."

She rolls away from me and sits up, sliding off the bed.

Stalling.

She picks up her panties from the floor and slips them on. Armoring up with clothing for her talk with me.

"Sloane."

She turns and looks at me with those stunning copper-brown eyes.

"Leave your clothes off. Come here." I pull the bedcovers back to offer her their shelter if she's cold.

But the moment of openness and trust is gone. She ignores my demand and walks back to the kitchen to get her t-shirt. She comes back with it on, although she left the bra off.

"What's the money for?"

She sighs and walks back to the bed, climbing under the covers, but never meeting my gaze.

I've been thinking about it a lot since she told me about her dad and how she ended up in Arizona. I even

Googled to read a couple news stories about his arrest and death.

"One of his associates… "

My attention sharpens to a point. Somehow I know whatever she's about to tell me is bad.

She swallows. "I think he's mafia. My dad was mixed up with him somehow. I don't know—it never came out in the court case against him.

"He showed up right after my dad died in jail, demanding his cut. He seems to think my dad had some assets that weren't seized by the FBI and that I would know where they are. They were going to kill me, or sell me, so I lied. I told him I still had boxes of his stuff and would find it all, but I seriously don't have a clue. The boxes were just clothes. I donated all of them and threw away any letters my dad sent from jail without opening them.

This guy told me he'd be gone to Sicily for a few months and said I needed to have it figured it out by the time he got back. I have no idea how much time I have left. In the meantime, his goons show up every week or so to lean on me.

"So I've been stealing cars and saving up. Hoping I can produce enough to mollify him when he comes back. Or make a run for it." Her voice chokes, and I reach for her, half certain she'll fight me off.

She lets me hold her, though. I lie down beside her and wrap her in my arms. She tucks her face against my chest. The scent of her tears does something crazy to me. Shreds my chest open. Makes my wolf want to howl.

"That's bullshit, Sloane. If you don't have the assets, you don't have them."

"I know, but I guess they think if they squeeze me hard enough I'll magically produce them. Last time they stopped by, they threatened to sell my cousin Rikki, too."

White hot rage mingles with icy dread flush my system at the same time, making my skin prickle and electricity crackle in my joints. "I'll fucking kill them," I growl, and I mean it.

I may have been horrified at what I did to the car jacker a few hours ago, but right now I'd be happy to murder for Sloane again. Over and over again until every threat against her is gone.

She tries to push away from me. "No. These guys are really dangerous. And it's probably a big network. I mean, the boss would just send someone else."

I go silent, my mind whipping around the problem. "How much do they say you owe them?"

"He says my dad had six gold bars the size of an iPhone and some little painting of a bird. I don't know what my dad was into with these guys or why they think I have this stuff. It's all just fuck-nuts crazy."

I hold her tighter. I can't believe she's been going through this shit alone.

"So I'm just trying to come up with anything I can give him. At first I sold off the few possessions I had that were worth anything—diamond earrings my dad gave me for my sixteenth. My mom's wedding ring. And then I decided stealing cars would be the easiest way to get money fast. But time's running out, and I've lost the last two cars." She chokes up again.

I curse because I don't know how we can come up with that kind of cash so fast.

"What happens if you go to the cops?"

"They'll kill my aunt and cousin. Or sell them to sick assholes to use as fuck dolls."

These fucking bastards. "Well... we'll figure it out."

"We? No, there's no we. Bo, I didn't tell you about this for a reason. I don't want you involved. They threaten anyone I'm close to. It's why I can't date. It's not safe."

I take her hand and push it down from my chest to the place the bullet went into me a few hours ago. "Feel that, Legs? That's what bullets do to me. Not much. I'm not afraid of them. I'm not going to let them push you around like this."

Despite my reassurances, Sloane's body has grown more and more tense, and now I detect a slight tremble in her limbs.

Fuck this. My wolf snarls inside, furious that anything would make Sloane shake with fear.

I squeeze her tight. "It's okay. We'll figure something out. I promise."

"I don't want your promise, Bo. This isn't your fight."

"It's not yours, either! That's the part that doesn't make sense. I really don't get why they're leaning on you. Do they really think a high school kid can generate that much cash? I mean, if the sex slave thing is real, why wouldn't they just do that from the start?"

"It's because they seem to think I have the money stashed somewhere. Which, of course, I don't. The FBI seized everything when they raided the house. All I took to Arizona was the stuff in my room—my clothes and personal effects. They took my car, my dad's car, the house, all his bank accounts—everything."

"When does your time run out?"

"I don't know. Soon—any day now."

"All right. We'll figure something out."

Sloane blinks back tears as she wraps her arms around my neck and squeezes too hard. Her breath makes her belly shudder against me. "Thanks," is all she manages to say.

"It's okay, beautiful. I promise. It's going to be okay," I say, even though I don't know how to make my words true. I hold her back tight and gently rock her until eventually she gets tired and lies down.

I turn out the light and listen to the sound of her breath as she falls into a fitful sleep.

Think, Bo, think. There has to be a way out of this for Sloane.

I gave her my word we'll figure it out, and that's what I'm going to do.

CHAPTER 12

loane

I WAKE up sore and scared and really fucking grateful for the guy beside me.

He wants to be my knight.

I want to let him.

I really want to let him.

But I just can't.

There's no way I'm going to allow him to put his life at risk for me.

I care about him too much.

My mom might lose both her sons. Over me. I can't have that.

The sooner I can get Bo to bring me back to Cave Hills and we go our separate ways, the better.

Or… maybe I should go jack another car right now. At

least I wouldn't show up to the meet empty-handed. They said they wouldn't accept a stolen car, but you never know. They have to have their own contacts for fencing that kind of thing. At least they'd know I was putting in my good faith effort.

I slip out of bed.

And am immediately greeted by the low rumble of Bo's voice. "You hungry?"

Dammit. He probably has super sensitive hearing or requires zero sleep. I wish I could grill him about the wolf thing, but he made it off-limits.

My stomach rumbles in answer to his question. "Yeah."

"I'm starving. Let's go find some breakfast." He gets up and pulls on jeans, foregoing the ripped boxer briefs.

"What are you going to do for a shirt?" I ask, pulling on my own jeans.

"Fuck. I don't know. Maybe there's something here." He opens the closet doors, but other than extra pillows and blankets, they're bare.

A knock sounds at the door, and it opens before Bo gets there. Jared and two other big guys come through the door. All three are covered in tattoos and leather, looking like a badass biker gang.

I wonder if all biker gangs are actually comprised of werewolves?

The smaller of the three—although small probably isn't a word anyone ever uses to describe him—carries a box of Krispy Kreme donuts and a gallon of milk. "You kids hungry?"

"Yeah, we were just going for food. Thanks," Bo says.

Jared tosses him a t-shirt. "We were afraid you were

thinking about squirreling out of here without saying goodbye, so we thought we'd head you off."

"No, sir," Bo says, addressing the biggest guy, rather than Jared. "This is my girlfriend, Sloane. Sloane, this is Garrett and Trey. They're all from my hometown."

I assume that's code for—*they're all wolves,* or *they're all from my pack,* but they don't know that I know, so I shake hands politely. "Nice to meet you."

Trey sets the box of donuts on the kitchen table, and Bo and I dive into them.

"So what happened last night?" Garrett pulls a chair back and sits in it. The other two also sit, and since there's only three chairs, Bo and I remain standing.

Like we're on trial.

Which we maybe are.

Bo gets out five glasses and pours the milk. "Sloane's in some trouble. It's personal to her, and I don't think you necessarily need to know what it is," he explains, and I breathe a sigh of relief.

"Does it involve the same trouble Winslow's in?" Garrett asks.

I stiffen.

Bo picks up his third donut. "Yeah, it's related. You guys heard about that, huh?"

"Member of the former pa—uh, community—gets shot by cops, yeah, we're gonna hear about it," Trey says.

Garrett narrows his eyes at Bo. "Were you involved in the car thefts?"

Bo squares his shoulders. "No, sir. Well, not until last night."

Garrett relaxes back in his chair and crosses one ankle over a massive knee. "Okay."

"Like I said, Sloane's in some personal trouble that isn't her fault. She needs a lot of money fast. That's how she got mixed up in stealing cars. Last night she tried to sell one to these assholes on the border, and they jacked the car instead. They tried to kill us, but, ah, we got away."

Garrett looks at Bo for a long time, then his glance darts at me.

I'm pretty sure he's trying to figure out if I know they're wolves or not.

"*How* did you get away?"

Bo shifts on his feet.

"You lie to me, I will beat your ass," Garrett warns.

Bo rubs his nose. The other men's gazes shift to me and back.

"Come on. You're better off telling me than you are my dad, so spill it."

"I shifted when they shot me."

Shifted. That's what they call it.

Bo's voice is quiet like he's admitting something bad. I know he said he violated two pack rules. I'm guessing revealing himself to non-werewolves was one of them. "There were three of them. I did some damage to one guy, but I don't think it was fatal. At least, he was alive when they left."

"*Fuck*," Garrett says.

Bo runs his hand through his hair. "Well, what the fuck was I supposed to do?" He drops his gaze again. "—sir."

"No, you did what any of us would do. You just shouldn't have been in that situation to begin with, but I'm guessing you already know that." Garrett takes one of the last donuts and puts half of it in his mouth.

"And the money?" Trey asks.

Bo shakes his head. "They took the car and the money —if they ever had any."

"So you're still in trouble, then." He directs this at me, and I straighten and nod. I'm not often out of my element, and when I am, I'm damn good at bluffing, but these guys intimidate me. I think it's knowing they aren't human. Not being clear on the code they live by.

Trey toys with the piercing in his lip. "There's a fight at two," he muses.

I have no idea what that means, but the rest of the guys in the room whip their heads around to stare at him.

"No way," Jared says. "You can't put a high school baller in a fight. Coach Jamison will come down here and put our asses in a sling if the alpha doesn't first."

"How old are you?" Trey asks Bo, ignoring Jared.

"Eighteen."

Trey shrugs. "He's an adult. He can make his own decisions." To Bo, he says, "You want to fight? If you win, it'll pay at least ten thousand, maybe more, depending on how the bets go."

"You think he can win?" Garrett asks doubtfully.

"It's actually because he's not full-sized yet, I think he can beat this guy. He's still fast. Light on his feet." He turns to Bo. "I have an asshole cat shifter who wants to fight. Bets will be on him because of your age and size."

"Then you take the fucker down," Jared tells Bo.

"Done." Bo rolls his shoulders, looking every inch the badass.

"I-I don't know," I say. "I don't want you risking yourself for—"

Bo holds up his hand. "It's not a risk." He lifts his shirt

to show me the place he got shot last night. It's completely healed. Hardly even a mark now.

I shake my head. "I still don't like it."

I don't. But I am turned on that he's willing to go in the ring for me. *Very* turned on.

Garrett stands, and the other two follow. "Step outside with me, Bo," he commands.

Bo darts a glance at me as he follows the men out of the apartment and shuts the door.

I stand there and blink for a moment.

Then I rush to press my ear against the door.

Bo

I FOLLOW Garrett into the hallway, willing my heart rate to stay steady. Fate knows an alpha will smell fear all over you if you let it in.

Fuck.

"So." Garrett folds his arms over his massive chest. "What are you going to do about the girl?"

I knew this was going to be about Sloane, even though I was praying to avoid the inevitable.

"She swore she'd take it to the grave," I say quickly. Like a human's promise means anything to these guys.

Garrett shakes his head slowly. "You know that's not good enough."

I want to argue with him. Garrett has a human for a mate. So does Jared, for that matter. Garrett was not cut from the same cloth as his father, other than being alpha enough to lead a pack. He and his friends were rebels. They were thrown out of our pack when they weren't much older than I am, and they do things their own way here.

Still, that doesn't mean he's going to cut me any slack.

The rules are in place to protect shifters from exposure. If humans found out we existed, we'd be hunted down and exterminated as monsters.

I rack my brain, trying to think of something I can say —anything—to spare Sloane the fate I'm pretty sure they're going to demand.

"Get her memory wiped tonight. It's twenty-four hours. It shouldn't have too bad an effect. I'll text you the number of a guy who can do it."

I shake my head. "We have to be back in Phoenix with the money by this evening."

Garrett pins me with a hard stare. "Then you bring her back here afterward. You know the rules. Don't fuck up."

Shit. Fuck. Damn it all to hell.

I turn to go back in the apartment without being dismissed, but Garrett throws me up against the door with his hand at my throat.

"I need to hear a *yes, sir.*"

Dammit. I really don't want to agree to having a vampire tamper with Sloane's mind. It can cause problems, and she doesn't deserve that kind of shit. But I don't see any way around this direct order. "Yes, sir," I choke.

He releases me. "Good." He pulls a couple bills from his pocket. "You need money before the fight?" He's a good alpha, aware of his pack members' needs.

I'm not one to turn money down, so I take the twenties and shove them in my pocket. "Thanks, Garrett."

He grunts, and the three start off down the hallway.

"Garrett?"

He turns.

"Are you going to tell your dad about this?"

He shakes his head. "My territory, my problem. You can decide for yourself what you want to tell your alpha."

"Thanks." I watch them walk away, feeling like a fifty pound weight is on my chest.

I don't begrudge Garrett for doing what an alpha is supposed to do to keep our species safe—but fuck.

Wiping Sloane would be a mega-betrayal. I mean, *fuck*. Should I tell her it's going to happen to minimize the fuck-over?

Is there any point when that conversation would be wiped, too?

Dammit!

I turn the knob and enter the apartment. The shower's running in the bathroom. For a moment, I consider joining Sloane for Act II of her birthday shower fucking, but guilt's strangling me like a parasitic vine. I decide to run out for toothbrushes and a razor, instead.

And maybe coffee or Dr. Pepper.

And a phone charger or both our phones will die.

I leave Sloane a quick note and head to the elevators.

I can't think about wiping Sloane's mind. First, I have to win a fight against a cat shifter. Then get her mafia assholes paid off. Then I can worry about what's next.

Yeah, because sticking my head in the sand always works well.

SLOANE

I BRUSH my teeth with the toothbrush Bo brought back, trying to act like everything's cool. Like I'm not totally freaked out about everything.

The fight.

The money.

The mafia.

Getting my memory wiped.

Because I heard what Garrett told Bo. *Get her memory wiped tonight.*

I don't know how that works, but I know I don't want it. I was stupid to trust anyone to have my back. No one ever has. I came into this world alone, and I'll go out alone.

I mean, I don't blame Bo. I recognized the tension in him from the moment I witnessed his secret. I'm not supposed to know. I get it.

And he's still a fucking knight in shining armor to me. He saved my life. He's going to fight to win money for me.

He has my undying gratitude.

But he's been right from the start. I'm bad news for him and his family. Now I'm going to cause him stress with his pack.

I definitely am not going to cause him trouble with the Detroit mafia, too.

As soon as this fight's over, I need to get out of here. Break things off with Bo. I can't have him acting like the hero to save my ass. I couldn't live with myself if something happened to him.

Bo bought a charger, and my phone's plugged in now. I

texted my aunt last night to tell her I was spending the night with a friend.

I'm pretty sure she knows that friend is Bo because she wrote back, *Please believe you can be honest with me. I just want you to be safe.*

I wrote, *I will be safe!*

I know, it's probably much less than she wanted, and I'll probably have to suffer through some kind of safe sex lecture when I get back.

"So...now what?" I ask Bo when we're both through brushing our teeth.

His expression is tight. "We have a couple hours to burn. I don't know—want to go see some of Tucson?"

My chest tightens even more. How is this guy so damn sweet?

"Yeah, that'd be nice." I lace my fingers through his, savoring every touch, every gesture as our last.

"Want to learn how to drive a motorcycle?" he asks when we get outside.

Some of the heaviness on my limbs lifts, and I almost manage a smile. "Totally."

Bo flashes that pirate grin at me, and for a moment, my heart flutters—happiness flitting its delicate wings—before I remember I don't get to keep this.

I don't get to keep him.

But I have these moments. The world sharpens into focus. The sun is already warming the cool autumn morning, and I'm with the guy who is sex on wheels. I put on the helmet and listen carefully as he explains how to hold in the clutch and kick the motorcycle to life. It takes me several tries—five to be exact—but I get it going.

Pirate grin.

Swoon.

"Okay, now you're going to practice putting it into gear. Have you driven a stick?"

I shake my head.

He swings his leg over the seat to sit on the bike behind me, reaching around to hold the handlebars.

For a moment, I stop listening, savoring instead the way his body snugs up against mine. His freshly-showered clean scent. The sight of his strong forearms and big hands.

I love you.

Those are the words that pop into my head.

I don't say them, of course.

I'll never say them. It wouldn't do either of us any good. But they're real and true.

He explains the gear shifting with the clutch and then demonstrates it a couple times before he lets me try.

I instantly kill the bike.

Dammit.

Three more tries to kickstart the engine. Four to get the bike in gear and moving.

Bo's arms stay loose around me, like he's ready to take over if I screw up, but we're off, putzing in first gear up the street.

"Now put the clutch in and change gear," he says in my ear.

Unbelievably, I do it.

I laugh as we pick up speed. I take us on the back streets near downtown, driving up and down through historical neighborhoods.

"Take a right here," Bo directs, pointing to a larger street. I follow his directions, and soon we're climbing a road that leads up a large hill—or maybe a small peak—with a giant letter "A" on it for the U of A.

The landscape in Arizona is unbelievably different from Michigan. At first, I saw it as all brown, but now that I've been here a few months, I see the color in the browns. The textures. The greens of the sahuaros, the glow of their spines at sunset—like a halo of light surrounding the giant cacti. There are wildflowers in autumn. And fruit on the cacti.

And now that the excruciating heat of summer is past, there's something cleansing about the sun. Like it will burn off all the shit in my life and make it new again.

We drive all the way to the top of the mountain, and I nearly kill us trying to park it. Not really, but Bo had to put his feet down and grab the handlebars to keep me from dumping it.

"Good job, Legs. You did it."

I hop on one leg to dismount and turn to face him. "I did." Despite everything we've been through and still face, I can't stop the smile from spreading across my face. "Thank you."

He takes me into his arms and just holds me there.

For once, the charge of sexual tension is absent. Or at least diminished. There's a sweetness to the way he holds me. Like he, too, knows this is our last day together.

That we should savor these small moments.

I don't know how long we stand there. It's a while.

Finally, Bo shifts on his feet and releases me. "We'd better get to Fight Club."

"Seriously? It's called Fight Club?"

"Shifter Fight Club, yeah."

I freeze as the realization hits me. "Oh shit. Is this like, cage fighting?"

"Yeah, definitely." I get a glimpse of the pirate grin. "Don't worry, I got this, Legs."

My stomach tightens into a hard knot.

I sure as hell hope he's right.

CHAPTER 13

o

I DEFINITELY DIDN'T KNOW what I was getting myself into.

I've been in fights. With my buddies. With other shifters my age.

Not with full-grown shifters of other species.

It's noon on a Sunday, but Shifter Fight Club is *packed.* I mean crazy-packed.

The smells alone overwhelm me. I've never seen so many different species of shifters. There are so many scents I can't identify.

Trey's girlfriend Sheridan struts around the place, giving orders and taking no prisoners. She's hot as hell, but I'm careful not to look. I scent Trey's mark on her, which means he could get very territorial and testy if he finds me disrespectful.

I have my own girl to protect, and my wolf is definitely riled up about all the possible dangers to her.

Too bad the worst one could be me.

I keep my hands at her waist, needing to feel her under me, to show my claim on her, even though she's not marked.

She gets a ton of looks, but most aren't friendly. They know she's human, and humans probably aren't allowed here. Or at least aren't welcome.

In typical Sloane fashion, she doesn't show any discomfort; she just tosses her hair and looks around coolly.

"I'm going to take Bo to the back, but you can stand behind the bar here, with Sheridan," Trey tells her.

"Sheridan, this is Sloane, Bo's girlfriend from Cave Hills."

Sheridan was princess of the Wolf Ridge pack before she left to slum it with Trey, so she knows exactly what that means. She studies Sloane for a half-second before extending her hand. "Nice to meet you. You can stick back here with me where you'll be safe while Bo fights. Sound good?"

Sloane nods. Again, she shows nothing, but I sense her unease. I give her hand a quick squeeze before I leave with Trey.

He gives me a pair of gym shorts to change into and a pep talk that I barely hear.

I've spotted my competitor, and he looks vicious. Bigger than me, but it's not so much his size as it is the nasty expression on his face I find daunting. Like he wants to disembowel me.

Hopefully, that hasn't happened here.

I jump around on the balls of my feet, listening to the roar of the crowd as the first fight gets underway.

Time speeds up. Or maybe it stands still. All I know is one minute I'm standing there waiting, the next minute, Trey is propelling me forward, into the cage, announcing my name and stats to the crowd.

I don't even see the first punch coming. It flattens me, possibly breaking my cheekbone.

I roll and spring up, though, faster than he expects, and circle the cat. I think he's a panther. No, maybe a jaguar. How the fuck do I know?

He jabs another punch, but I dodge this one. Try my own. I catch him in the ribs, but then he catches me, too.

We circle each other, throwing a few punches. I dodge the first two, then take a blow to the temple that drops me. My vision goes black. I don't know for how long—maybe a second. I scramble back up, but the crowd is booing me.

The cat is laughing. He comes at me again. I'm dizzy, and I misjudge my punch, sending it wide. I take another one to the teeth and stumble back.

He advances. "You fighting for that girl you came with?" he taunts. "That pretty little piece of pussy?"

I growl. I know he's trying to get rise out of me, but I can't fucking help myself. I don't like him talking about Sloane.

"Think she's impressed with her little high school boyfriend right now?" he cackles. "I'm pretty sure she's over there peeing her pants. Why the fuck would you bring a human to a place like this?"

He swings again, and I dart in, punching him square in the gut four times before he gets me back.

"Tell you what, wolfie. Let's make a deal. If I win, I'll

give you my prize money if you let me take your pretty human for a ride."

That's it. I barely hold my wolf back as I lunge for him. I tackle him to the ground and pin him, punching his face over and over again. He stands no chance of getting free now. My brain's only focused on one intent: to protect my female.

And to punish any threat to her.

I don't even notice when he goes unconscious, only that Trey has to yank me off him, shouting, "Enough, Bo! It's over—you won!"

SLOANE

TREY HOLDS Bo's fist in the air as champion, and the crowd roars—mostly disapproval, I think, but all the wolves are for Bo, and they shout the loudest.

Bo's gaze cuts through the crowd to land on me, and he grins, blood showing through his teeth just like it did the night of the homecoming dance.

Jesus.

My palms are sweaty and cut open from my fingernails stabbing into the flesh I was so scared. And he's up there grinning. Like he just had the time of his life.

Crazy freaking wolf boy.

I'm nearly bowled over by the rush of emotion that fills my chest. Love, I guess. Total affection. Gratitude. Maybe they're all the same thing.

I love that wolf boy standing up there, grinning because he just fought for me and won.

Trey drags him through the back entrance, and he disappears, then resurfaces in a fresh t-shirt and his jeans, pushing through the crowd to me. I come out from behind the bar and throw myself at him.

He laughs, catching me around the waist then hoisting me higher, so I straddle his waist.

"You were incredible," I shout, dropping kisses on his neck, biting his shoulder.

"I almost D.Q.ed," he says.

"What do you mean?"

"It's against the rules to let your animal out in the cage, and I damn near sprouted fangs to kill the fucker."

My thighs tighten around his waist as the hot room spins around me. There's so much otherworldly stuff to take in here, I am still reeling.

My boyfriend is a wolf.

Fake boyfriend.

Or is he real now?

"He disrespected you, and I went nuts," Bo tells me.

I want to screw him right here. This wolf-knight thing turns me on like nothing in the world. He must get the vibe because his arms tighten around me. He heads for the back room where he came from.

I see people settling up their bets as we walk through—cash being paid out by a grey-haired man with a young face flanked by a taller man with Coke-bottle glasses and a man shouting directions to the bettors in an Irish brogue.

"Employees only—oh, it's you," the huge guy guarding the door to the back says. His gaze travels from my face to Bo, and then he sighs and steps aside. "Tell me you have protection," he rumbles at Bo.

Jesus, is it that obvious? My face grows warm. Actually, it was already warm. It's probably stop sign red now.

"Yep, I'm good," Bo calls back to him. He carries me into the storeroom and sits me on a stack of boxes. "Sorry—that was lame. Are you embarrassed? We don't have to do this."

I must still be blushing, but I don't care. I don't know that guy or anyone else here. And I want to show Bo my appreciation.

"I'm harder than stone for you, Legs. Feel it."

I grab a handful of his cock through his jeans and squeeze hard. "Take it out." My voice sounds husky.

"Fates," he mutters, unbuttoning his jeans fast, like his life depends on it.

I move to slide off the box and get on my knees, but he catches me, turning me around to face the boxes and smacking my ass. "I want to be inside you." He reaches around the front and rubs between my legs. "Is that okay, beautiful?"

"Yeah." I consider telling him to be gentle because I'm still sore from last night and from getting punched in the ribs, but I don't actually want him to be gentle.

I like it when it hurts a little.

I like it when he's rough.

I like sensing the animal in him. To see him out of control with desire for me. The way his eyes change color—now I understand why they sometimes look silver.

I'm already wet for him. I cover his hand with mine and urge him on. He nuzzles my neck, his breath hot, his teeth scraping over my skin. He unbuttons my jeans and slides his hand in. I moan the minute his digits touch my sensitive bits, my pelvic floor contracting.

"Oh fates, Sloane. You're so wet."

"Fuck me, wolf boy."

His movements gain urgency. He shoves my jeans and panties down and gives my ass a hard smack. If you'd asked me before if I wanted a guy to slap my ass, the answer would have definitively been no, but every time he does it, I get more excited. And I'm already burning with lust for him.

I hear the rustle of his pants, the snap of foil and then feel the prod of his sheathed cock at my entrance. I push back to welcome him. I'm sore from last night but also so ready, and he slides right in, the soreness only making the pleasure, the rightness, more delicious.

"Sloane," he rasps, his fingers wrapping around my hips, his cock stretching me wide, filling me on each slow stroke. "You feel so good."

I look over my shoulder at him, and he claims my mouth in a sloppy, sideways kiss.

"You're so fucking hot. I don't see how a human could be this hot."

I'm absurdly pleased by that praise, even though it's a backhanded compliment. "You're the only one," I tell him.

"The only what?"

"The only one who's been here." He knows that already—that he took my virginity—but I'm trying to tell him something else. "The only one I let in. The only one I trusted."

I meant I *can trust,* but it came out past tense. Because I already know he's supposed to wipe my memory, clear the past twenty-four hours from my brain.

His movements stutter, like he heard my slip, and he's wondering if I know.

He lets out a curse and starts fucking me hard, bringing one hand round to rub my clit. He's bringing us to a finish already.

The metaphor isn't lost on me.

It's what needs to happen.

I close my eyes and surrender to the intensity of his thrusts. A few more seconds, and I come, my body convulsing, my channel tightening and squeezing his cock.

He growls and slams harder, harder, harder until he shoves in deep and stays, his breath holding and catching, then releasing on a low, slow growl.

He's wearing a condom, but I swear I feel the heat of his release inside me, and my muscles squeeze and twitch around him some more. Bo rubs my clit and gets a few more shudders out of me before he pulls out and pulls up my panties. There's something hot about him reaching around to zip and button my jeans. Hot and sweet.

He kisses my neck. I don't look at him. I can't. It's time to put walls back up. Re-erect my barriers, say goodbye to this incredible guy I want to keep forever.

"Hang on, I'll be right back." He disappears to dispose of his condom and returns with a bottle of water, which he cracks and offers to me.

I drink deeply and hand it back.

"Bo? I have your payout," Trey calls, clearly giving us space in case he's interrupting something. "Come on in my office."

Bo grabs my hand, and we jog out.

"I'm going to run to the ladies room," I tell him. "Meet you in the bar?"

He squeezes my hand. "Sounds good."

I go to the restroom, then head out to the bar. It's emptied of three-quarters of the people, but I instantly recognize the figure sitting at the bar.

Winslow.

And he's not happy to see me. Not at all.

The guy still scares me, even now that Bo and I are an item, but I square my shoulders and walk over to him. "Hey. I'm glad to see you're okay. Your family's been worried."

He narrows his eyes at me.

"I told you to keep him the fuck out of it."

"I know. I did. At least, I tried. He's a hard guy to put off, though."

I forgot how big a guy he is. Bo seems big, but this guy towers over me, and he's built like a tank. It's hard not to flinch when he leans down and gets right in my grill. "I heard there was trouble last night. And I'm one hundred percent sure it was your doing. So I'm only going to tell you this once: get the fuck out of Bo's life."

I'm shocked by the sudden urge to cry. Like I have to blink quickly to clear the water from my eyes. "I will," I warble. Because that's been my plan all along.

"If you don't, I will turn you in to the cops as my accomplice on the stolen cars."

He probably won't because that would mean turning himself in, too, and I doubt he plans to do that, but I experience the threat viscerally, a wash of adrenaline kicking through me.

"It's already done. I'm leaving," I say, as Bo appears behind me.

"Winslow." He looks past Winslow at the guy sitting

next to him. "Ben." Surprise and a little indignation ring in Bo's voice. It's not the happy reunion I might have expected. I sense tension radiating from him, and he slips something into the waistband of my jeans in the back—must be the envelope of money—like he doesn't want Winslow to see it.

"Is this where you've been? Mom's been worried sick about you. For fuck's sake, you could've called."

Winslow's face contorts in anger. "That's pretty ripe coming from the kid who might've killed a man last night."

I take a step back, and Bo steps in front, as if to shield me from Winslow. His friend climbs up from his seat, like he has Winslow's back. They look about the same age. And IQ. "Hey, go and wait for me at the bike," he murmurs, patting my leg.

Don't have to ask me twice.

I leave the building—a warehouse that's been converted into a hip, industrial bar and stand out in the newly paved parking lot.

It takes me a few moments for my situation to sink in and then everything snaps into place.

It's time for me to make good on my promise to Winslow. To leave.

Without Bo.

CHAPTER 14

o

Son of a *fucking* bitch!

I kick the side of the metal warehouse that houses Fight Club, my stomach stuck up under my ribs making it hard to breathe.

She left.

She fucking took the money *and my bike*...and left.

That *bitch!*

No, I don't mean that.

Yes, I do.

Fuck!

I kick the building again, denting the metal and probably breaking a couple toes in the process. I can't believe I just got played by Sloane McCormick. I mean, what the actual fuck?

I throw the door open and step back inside, blinking as

my eyes adjust to the change in light. Winslow's still at the bar.

Really, I can't believe that fucker, either. The whole time he was kicking it down here in Tucson with the rest of the wolves banished from our pack. I should've known he'd be just fine. The pack elders try to drill it into our heads that we wouldn't survive without a pack. Lone wolves are in danger and all that shit. Here I was so worried about Winslow being banished, and he's been just fine. Turns out, he already has a job working for Tank, another former Wolf Ridge pack member who has a motorcycle shop here.

He's not starving and alone, wandering the human populace with none of his own kind around him.

And I'm an idiot for even caring.

I stomp over to him, pick up his beer and drain it.

He looks over at me with an indulgent grin. Yeah, pretty much our relationship in the last few years has consisted of him buying me and my friends beer because we're not old enough yet.

"She's gone. She took my fucking bike and left. Do you have wheels?"

"Good riddance," Winslow says easily. Almost like he expected it.

I narrow my eyes. Shouldn't he be pissed on my behalf that she stole the Triumph? I mean, he didn't like her to begin with.

Winslow orders another beer. "Tank let me borrow a truck. But I need it."

"Alpha Green said you had to show up to council or be banished."

"Fuck him," Winslow says.

I'm not surprised by that answer.

"Well, at least drive me home, go see Mom and relieve her mind about you."

He raises his brows. "You paying for gas?"

Right, with all the money I don't have, since *Sloane just took it all*. But I don't have any option but to agree. "Yeah."

He sighs and stands up, taking the beer the bartender brings him and chugging it. "Let's go."

I don't speak the entire way home. I'm pissed at Winslow, and I'm pissed at Sloane. But mostly I'm just pissed at myself.

Why the fuck *did* I ever get involved in this bullshit? Because a hot pair of legs walked into the shop at full moon, and I'm still such a teenage horndog I couldn't stop chasing?

What a fucking idiot.

I try not to think about any of it but instead end up examining every moment we spent together.

The first ride on my bike. Her paying me to teach her to drop an engine, then realizing it's too much to pick up on the fly.

Her Homecoming dance.

Getting her off with the vibrator.

Sex.

That part was real. Fates, but I have to believe that part was real. This hasn't all been a hustle.

And she wasn't hustling me because I was the goddamn pursuer.

Didn't stop her from using me, though, did it?

From letting me fight for her. Taking the money I earned her.

She's desperate, the little whisper of reason reminds me.

Yeah, but I was right by her side the whole time. Protecting her. Keeping her from doing this alone. Hopefully coming up with some way to solve this bullshit she's caught in.

Only she didn't want me to be her knight in shining armor.

The rejection burns a tree trunk sized hole through the center of my chest. I really fucking cared about this girl, and she crumpled me up like a used piece of paper and tossed me in the trash.

I would've done anything for her.

And as that thought descends and lands, I feel it through all my limbs. Through every organ, through every blood cell moving in my veins.

I still would.

Even after her betrayal, I still would.

~

Sloane

I cry the whole way back to Wolf Ridge. I feel like an asshole leaving Bo with his dick swinging in the wind. And I'm a selfish bitch because I really I don't want to do this thing alone. It may have only been twenty-four hours, but I sure as hell liked having Bo on my side. Picking up the sword and fighting my battles for me.

But, of course, I can't let him.

And I'm going to have to keep bitching him over if I want him to stay away.

I ride his motorcycle to Wolf Ridge Body Shop, which

fortunately, appears to be closed. I open the envelope of money and count it out. Eleven thousand seven hundred dollars.

That's a pretty amazing take for a high school kid on a single day.

I wish I could leave it all for him. And I would, if I wasn't also worried about my cousin. Instead, I leave him the seven hundred and take the eleven grand. I dig in my purse for a pen and write on the back of a receipt:

Bo,

Forgive me for ending things this way.

Please don't come looking for me. I'll pay you back when I can.

Thanks is definitely not enough, but it's all I have.

And I know you owe me nothing, but I have one more favor to beg: please don't wipe my memories of you. I need them.

—S

I WANT to write *I love you,* but it's the wrong thing to do. It would open a door instead of close one. And I can't have Bo in my life anymore.

I wipe my tears with my fingers and stuff the note and cash in the envelope to tuck in his saddlebag. Hopefully no one will steal it before he finds it, but I sort of doubt they will. After that small glimpse of the shifter community in Tucson, I have a feeling everyone in Wolf Ridge looks out for one another. They aren't stealing money from each other.

Then I text the number I have for Vinny. I'm going to try to head off disaster by making a good faith payment of everything I have. I name a meeting place on a very public block in Scottsdale and call for a Lyft. I can stop at my aunt's to get the rest of the cash I have from the first car sale. Thirty grand should buy me a little more time.

As I ride to Cave Hills and then Scottsdale, my stomach churns on emptiness. My body feels half-dead. No—make that all dead. Because I'm starting to wonder what the point of living is with all I've given up.

I thought I'd stopped living when my dad went to jail and I came to Arizona, but I was wrong. I never even knew living. I didn't know it until Bo Fenton climbed in through my window and invaded my life. Declared himself my made-up boyfriend. Took me to Homecoming. Claimed my V-card and jumped in front of a firing gun for me.

And now that I know it, anything less than life with Bo is barely an existence.

But there's no helping it. Even if my situation wasn't seriously fucked—which it is—he can't be with me anyway. I heard what the pack leader in Tucson ordered. He plans to have my mind wiped of what he is. That means he couldn't be with me long term anyway.

Better now than after we have more time invested in each other. More of our hearts exposed and open for bludgeoning.

I make a quick stop at the townhouse, grateful my aunt and Rikki aren't home to ask questions, then get back in the car. The Lyft driver pulls up at the designated corner, and I get out, clutching my bag with the cash. I look around, but don't see the guys.

A whistle makes me look down the alleyway.

Fuck.

Of course they're parked there, where no one will see

this go down. I walk over and climb in the open door to the back seat. Tom climbs in beside me and shuts the door, and the car takes off down the street.

That was my first warning that something was wrong.

The second was the blow I take to the temple, which makes everything instantly go black.

Bo

WINSLOW and my mom sit at the kitchen table, my mom crying, Winslow covering her hand with his and promising everything will be all right.

I leave them to it and head down the hall to my room, where I flop face down on my bed.

All I feel is emptiness.

I should be happy. I accomplished the goal I set out to complete—find Winslow. Get him home to say goodbye to our mom. But there's zero satisfaction.

For one thing, goodbye is pretty irrelevant when Winslow is living two and a half hours away in Tucson. He may be hiding from the law, but he's not in a cave in Utah or out in New Mexico, off the grid, where some shifters go to disappear. He's in the next city over. With a job and a pack to take care of him.

But none of this is about Winslow.

It's about what went down with Sloane.

That girl fucking *destroyed* me.

I don't even know how it happened. I was calling all

the shots. I bum-rushed her life. But here I am, the one who's fucking shredded.

And she walked away unscathed.

Or did she?

I've checked my phone fifty times, but there's no message from her, and I'm still too pissed to send one myself. If I did, it would further destroy everything we were, and despite it all, I'm not sure I want that.

My phone buzzes, and I yank it out of my pocket. It's Wilde, checking on me: *You coming to school tomorrow, asshole?*

I ignore the text and close my eyes.

Will myself to fall asleep.

Hope to fate I'll feel more like myself in the morning.

That I'll know what to do.

I guess one thing is sure—I don't have to feel bad about getting Sloane's memories wiped. Not when she cares so little about me.

Sloane

My head throbs. I think I've been drugged because my body won't move. My mouth tastes like cotton, and I want to puke.

I'm sprawled across the back seat of the Navigator, and the beat I hear is the stereo blasting Post Malone. There's talking from the front seat, too, but I can't make out what they're saying over the music.

And it's day time.

Which means we've been driving all night. At least, I think we have. I gained consciousness a few other times during the night, and every time it was the same. The car moving. My body too sluggish to respond to commands.

Where in the hell are we going?

Oh fuck.

They're taking me to my new owner to be tortured and raped until… until what? I'm killed or sold again to someone else to repeat the same fate. Bile fills my throat, and I try to swallow it down.

At least Rikki isn't here, too. That would've killed me.

I cough, gagging a bit, and one of the guy's faces comes into focus where he's looking back at me. Tom. "She's awake again."

"Take care of her," Vinny says.

"What if she needs to go to the bathroom or something? I don't want her doing it in the car. I mean, how's it work with this shit?"

"Just give her another fucking shot!" Vinny snarls.

I try to make my lips move. "I do have to pee," I manage to croak. It's probably true. I can't really tell because I can't feel my body. But I definitely want them to stop somewhere, so I can get away.

"*Fanculo,*" Vinny snarls. Probably some Italian curse. The vehicle brakes suddenly and comes to a stop.

Well, shit.

I was kinda hoping for a rest stop. Or gas station. Or some other place besides the side of the road.

Tom gets out and throws open my door, hauling me out. My legs buckle beneath me, and I fall to the ground. He stares down at me with contempt. "Well, pee, then."

I'm sure I do have to pee. I work hard to get my hands

to move and manage to unbutton my jeans and pull them down. I hobble up to a squat and release my bladder.

Cornfields.

We're surrounded by cornfields. Which means... we're somewhere in the midwest.

Unexpected.

But I'm sure they need sex slaves everywhere.

I slowly stand and get my pants back up, but there's no time to button them before Tom shoves me back in the Navigator. "Water?" I croak. I'm so freaking thirsty.

"Give her another fucking shot," Vinny orders from the driver's seat.

"I am. Do you think she needs water, though? I mean, how long can a person go without drinking? It's been, like sixteen hours."

Sixteen hours. I've been out for a long time.

"I need water," I repeat.

"You give her water, she'll have to pee again. We can't risk it."

"Please," I beg. "Just a swallow."

Tom comes at me with a needle and jabs it in my arm. He slams my door and climbs back in the front seat. The vehicle peels out. The last thing I remember is him handing me back a bottle of water, but I never get it to my mouth.

~

Bo

. . .

"FENTON, DROP AND GIVE ME TWENTY!" Coach Jamison yells at me during practice when the ball hits me in the head. "Get your head out of your ass and show me and your teammates some respect!"

"Yes, sir!" I yell, but it's just mechanical. I'm answering by rote. I hardly register what he said or what he wants from me. I'm fifty fathoms under water right now, and I don't know which way to swim for air.

I don't even know what I'm feeling, other than that everything is wrong.

I'm pissed at Sloane. Pissed at myself. Pissed at the world. And deep down is the gnawing sensation that I need to find my way out of this coffin I'm stuck in, but I don't have a clue how to do it.

Somehow, I make it through practice.

"What's going on with you, Bo? Any word from Winslow?" Wilde asks in a low voice in the locker room. I expected him to give me shit for fucking up practice so much today, and the question helps pull some of the cotton out of my ears. Especially when the rest of the alpha-holes—Austin, Cole and Slade crowd around me to hear the answer.

I throw my hands in the air. "He's just been chillin' in Tucson. Right along with Ben Thomasson and the rest of the banished pack."

Ben Thomasson was banished after it came out that he bit Bailey, Cole's human girlfriend during the full moon run.

Cole snorts. "Figures. That dick is too cocky to hide or lay low. No offense."

I shake my head. Definitely none taken. My buddies

have been subject to Winslow and Ben's tyranny for as long as I have, which means all of our lives.

"What about Gone in Sixty Seconds?" Slade asks.

I shove him up against the lockers, my hand at his throat. "Don't call her that."

"Okay, take it easy, bro."

I don't want to let him go. I'd prefer to kill him. Just for mentioning her. For thinking about her.

Austin and Wilde each grab one of my arms and haul me back. "Dude. Chill. Will you chill?" Wilde gets his face right up to mine to growl the words.

I'd rather fight Slade. I'd rather fight them all.

But I probably won't feel any better.

I go slack then shake them off. "I need a ride home," I mutter.

"Why, did she steal your bike?" Cole scoffs.

I'm on him in an instant, tackling him to the ground. Cole is a mean motherfucker, especially with what's been going on in his home the last couple of years, but that doesn't stop me for a second. I want blood, and I want it now.

It takes Austin, Wild and Slade to pull me off him, and the whole time, they're whisper shouting because Coach is in the locker room now and will bust all of our asses if he catches us fighting.

They end up sitting on me—Wilde on my chest, Austin on my stomach, Slade on my legs. They sit on me until my vision changes back to normal, and I sag in defeat.

"Did she really steal your bike?" Wilde asks mildly.

This time I don't feel like fighting. I need my friends to help me understand what the fuck I'm navigating here. I nod.

Wilde whistles and climbs off me. The other two move and help me to my feet. "What are you going to do?"

I shrug. "I really don't know."

They all stare at me. I can't imagine why I thought they'd be any help.

"Well… I can't hurt her." Can't and wouldn't. Not ever. "I guess I'm gonna go fuck her."

It's stupid and reductionist, but the moment I say it, I feel a hundred ton weight shift off my chest.

Like my wolf is celebrating that I'm going to her. That fucking her is still on the table. That I'm not walking away.

Cole thumps me on the back. "That will definitely fix it, dude."

I can't tell if he's being sarcastic or real, but it doesn't matter. The lightness has taken over my body. I need to see Sloane. Fuck her senseless as punishment.

Then figure our shit out.

It's the only solution that makes any sense.

"Give me a ride to the shop," I say to Wilde, pulling my backpack out of my locker and slinging it on my back. "I gotta get Winslow's car to drive down to Cave Hills."

My heart stutters as we pull up to the shop. My bike is parked in the back, and I scan the area like maybe she's here, too.

I jump out of the Jeep and wave Wilde off, then run for the bike. The keys aren't in the ignition. I search the saddle bag and find them, along with the envelope of money I got from Trey. And a note.

I'm breathing hard as I read it.

And re-read it.

Bring it to my nose to sniff it. I smell her tears. That shouldn't be possible, but I swear it's true. Sloane was crying when she wrote this.

She fucking loves me. *Don't erase my memories of you. I need them.*

Everything snaps into place and becomes crystal clear.

She overheard about the memory wipe, so she ran. Who knows, maybe Winslow threatened her when they were alone, too. Yeah, knowing him, he probably did. And she'd been worried about me getting involved with her mafia problem.

So she cut me loose. She wasn't being a cunt. She cared. Cares.

And she didn't sell my bike. It was sweet of her to leave me a little of the money, too. Pocketing it, I get on my bike and start it.

If she thinks she gets to call the shots with me, she is sorely mistaken.

I drive to her aunt's townhouse and go with the old-fashioned method of knocking on the door.

Her aunt answers the door, and I'm unprepared for the blast of tension that erupts from her. "Bo!" She looks past me. "Where's Sloane?"

I look behind me, even though I know she won't be there. "What do you mean? She's not here?"

Her aunt bursts into tears. "She's been missing since Saturday. I thought she was with you... she never came home, and now she's not answering her texts."

Shock flashes through me. Like in a horror film, where they play the sudden blast of screechy music.

"Fuck." I stride into her aunt's house, not even apologizing for the bad language. I pull out my phone, as if it might magically have messages from Sloane on it now, and my hand shakes as I hold it.

"She didn't come home last night? Not at all since Saturday?"

"No. I've already called the police. They won't do an amber alert because she's over eighteen. I don't know—they don't seem to be taking it that seriously." Her aunt's voice breaks again.

I walk in and pace the small living room, eating it up with my long strides. "She was with me until yesterday afternoon, and then she left." I stop and run my hand through my hair.

Something bad has happened.

Something really bad.

And while it's not my story to tell, I can't keep her aunt in the dark any more about Sloane's problems.

"She's in some trouble," I manage to say. "Let's sit down. I'll tell you what I know."

Sloane's aunt drops onto the couch, and Rikki sits beside her. I sit on the edge of an armchair and start to tell the story. I get to the part about following her to Naco when I leap to my feet and whip my phone out. "I put a tracking app on her phone. Fates, maybe it's still on. Please let it still be on." My thumb skims across the screen on my phone, opening the app. I suck in a harsh breath when I see the bubble with her name.

"*Michigan*. She's in Michigan."

"Do you think she went to see this mafia guy?"

The room swoops around me. "Or they took her back there. They seemed to believe she had their stuff. Like she was hiding it or had already cashed out something. I guess she threw away her dad's letters without opening them, so we'll never know if he told her before he died."

Sloane's aunt's mouth opens, her eyes wide. "The letters!" She suddenly surges up to her feet. "She never opened them! I would find them in her garbage, unopened, and I pulled them out and saved them. I kept thinking one of these days she'd be ready or need closure and want to know what was in those letters. I tried to bring it up when he died, but she literally got up and walked away from me any time I mentioned him."

"So you still have them?"

She leaves the room without answering and returns with five envelopes. Rikki, Aunt Jennifer and I each begin tearing them open and skimming.

"I think I found it," Jennifer says, her voice rising as she reads, *If anything happens to me, check the storage locker 2238 at the EZ Storage by your old middle school. The key is on the ring with your bike lock.*

"I'll get the key!" Rikki jumps up and runs out of the room to the garage.

"I'm going to Michigan," I declare. "Sloane is there, and she needs my help." I pull the wad of cash out of my back pocket and thrust it at Jennifer. "But I don't have a credit card. Would you book me a flight?"

"I'm going, too," she says.

She's an adult, but the alpha in me has to overrule. "Nope. No way. Sloane didn't want you and Rikki involved."

"She's my niece. And you're just a kid," she says indignantly, although she has to look up—way up—to meet my eyes.

I shake my head. "I'm eighteen, and I can handle myself." I thrust the money Sloane left for me at her.

She sighs and walks past me, not taking the money. "You won't be able to rent a car!" she calls over her shoulder as she heads down the hall.

"I'll figure something out."

Rikki reappears with the keys. "Here they are." She hands them to me.

"Bo? Get in here," Jennifer calls from the kitchen, and I follow her in. "I need your full name. And put your phone number in my phone right now—and your mother's. And I'm going to require hourly updates."

"Yes, ma'am."

She looks over her shoulder with a wobbly smile. "I'm glad Sloane has someone like you, Bo."

Her words fortify the rod that runs down the very center of me. Like she's speaking to my very purpose in life.

Hell, maybe it is. If only Sloane would let me.

SLOANE

I WAKE up in a dim room—a warehouse, maybe—because there's concrete under my feet and lots of space overhead. I'm tied to a chair and my head hurts so badly I can't think.

"Hello, Sloane." A familiar smooth voice says. A salt-and-pepper haired man in an expensive suit appears in front of me. Mafia don. I missed when he got there.

I blink, trying to bring him into focus.

"You haven't delivered on your promise." He strokes my cheek with the back of my fingers and chills run down my spine.

My heart hammers in my chest. "I-I just need a little more time. I thought I had another week or two. I'm still working on it."

He backhands me across the face and my neck wrenches with the impact, stars dance in front of my eyes. "You're not working on it. You're screwing around stealing cars. I have my own car theft rings. I don't need a teenager to reinvent one. Now I'm back, and I want my gold."

"Here's what she had on her, Don Salvatore," Vinny says. "She brought thirty grand in cash."

Don Salvatore. Now I have a name to put with the nasty face. Salvatore takes my purse and rifles through. He pulls out my phone. "You left her phone on?"

"She never touched it, Don. She was out the whole time."

"People can be traced through phones, you idiot," he growls. "And her fucking location setting was on."

I sit up straighter. *Location setting.* Bo was tracking me before. Could he still be?

Probably not.

Definitely not after I told him we were through.

But however slim a chance there is, I find myself fixating on that sliver of hope. There's a chance I could be found. My aunt would've called the cops by now.

Maybe they're tracking my phone.

Salvatore takes the cash out and looks at it with disinterest. "I've been patient with you. Extremely patient. But I'm starting to think I didn't apply enough pressure. I told you to find the fucking gold and the painting. *So where is it?"*

I jerk in my chair at the sheer volume and closeness. His breath smells like sour coffee.

"I'm trying to find it!" I protest and get slapped across the face. And least it wasn't the backhand. That fucking hurt.

"Work her over," he orders, walking away.

~

Bo

LOTS of freaking firsts for me today. I've never been out of Arizona. Never flown on a plane before. Never taken an Uber.

It's all easy, though, because I'm in warrior mode. Ready to tear those assholes apart when I get to them.

I stride through the EZ Storage complex with the key out, seeking the right unit. I had to sign in and show I.D. and the key to the locker, but no one stops me from entering. This place isn't Fort Knox. If there are assets hidden here, the only thing keeping them safe is the fact that the storage unit was under the name S. MacCormac—spelled totally wrong—and that no one knew about it.

I find the right number, and the key to the corrugated metal unit fits and turns. I shut the door behind me for privacy, even though there's no light inside.

There are a few filing boxes. Three paintings wrapped up in moving blankets, including the small one of a bird. And a little briefcase-sized fire safe that's locked. I try the key to the storage unit on it, a puff of relieved laughter escaping my lips when it actually turns.

For once in this whole convoluted story, something's going right.

I open the lid and my body reacts to the sight of what's inside before my mind does.

Bars of gold. Slender, iPhone-sized bars of gold. Way more than the six Sloane said the mafia guy demanded from her. There's—I do a quick count—actually close to thirty. Which means Sloane's college tuition problem has also been solved.

If she's still alive, and I can get to her.

~

SLOANE

OH GOD, it's torture time. I may have once thought of myself as strong, but I'm pissing my pants right now.

"Wait!" I call to Don Salvatore. I don't know if that gold still exists somewhere I can get to it or not, but I do need to buy time.

"I have more money for you," I lie. "A good faith payment. Fifteen grand. M-my friend has it. He can bring it. Let me call him."

It's wrong to involve Bo. Very wrong. But if I can just get this message to him, maybe he can call the cops. Track me and get some help. Does tracking even work after locations have been turned off? I can only pray it does.

Salvatore cocks his head with a frown. I don't think he believes me, but he's greedy enough to entertain me. He pulls out my phone and turns it back on. It can't have more than one percent battery left on it. "Contact?"

I clear my throat.

Dammit, do I really want to do this? What if they kill me and go after Bo? But I don't see what other chance I have. "Bo."

Salvatore dials the number and puts it on speaker phone, holding it up to my face.

"Sloane." The urgency in Bo's voice tells me he knows I'm missing.

I almost weep with relief at hearing that strong, clear note.

"Hey, Bo," I speak fast. "Remember that money—th-that money that I had that belonged to someone else?"

"I have it."

I'm momentarily stunned by his clipped and unexpected answer. It's like he knew exactly what lie I just told and how to back it up.

"Y-you do?"

"Yeah, your aunt saved your dad's letters to you, and we figured it out. Where are you?"

My brain's moving too slowly to understand what he's saying. He figured it out? Where the gold is? I don't know how that's even possible, but hope—that dangerous winged creature in my chest—starts trying to fly.

I'm also struck by the dangerous edge to his voice. I remember he uses anger to mask fear, and I can't stop the tears of gratitude that leak from my eyes.

Salvatore's grin is pure evil. He takes the phone off speaker and walks away. "Where are *you*?"

I can't hear Bo's answer beyond the muffled sound of his rough tones.

"2915 N. 45th. There's a warehouse there. Meet me in forty minutes," Salvatore says. Satisfaction is written across his face.

Forty minutes? Is Bo here? In Michigan? He must've come to get the gold. Or for me.

This guy is beyond heroic. Beyond capable. Beyond anything I deserve or could ever ask for.

And he did all this for me.

Tears stream down my face.

"Call the Russian and pick up the girl," Salvatore says to Vinny and Tom. "He already paid for her."

"Wait!" Panic slams through me. "Aren't you taking me along? To trade for the gold?"

He leaves with another cluster of assholes dressed in suits and packing heat. The door slams.

Fuck!

I say a prayer on auto-loop: *please don't kill Bo. Please don't kill Bo. Please let us both get out of this alive.*

~

Bo

I HAVE a hard time not shifting. All the adrenaline dumping into my bloodstream makes my wolf want to come out and tear throats.

Soon.

I have to keep my head for now, though. Have to get Sloane safe.

I put the painting and gold bars in my backpack and start hoofing it to the meeting location, since I don't have my own wheels. At first I think it's the same location Sloane's phone last registered before it went off, but it's about a mile away.

I don't let myself think of the things that they might've done to her by now. If I do, I'll shift and rip my clothes right off.

I find the warehouse, but there's no one around, so I lean my back against the cold metal wall to wait. Five minutes later, a souped-up Caddy shows up. The windows are tinted—probably bullet-proof windows. I can't see if Sloane's inside or not. The back door opens, and an older dude in a suit steps out. Two other guys come out and flank him.

It was hard to tell, but when I looked in, I swear there was no one else in the car. I step closer, trying to scent her. Trying to see in.

My gut tells me she's not there, though.

Fuck! I knew I should've gone to the address she last showed up instead of this stupid meet location.

"Where's Sloane?" I demand.

"Show me the goods."

I unzip my backpack and show him the bars of gold and the painting. His eyes take on a greedy gleam that should've tipped me off to his next move, but I'm not worrying about him, I'm freaking about Sloane.

"Where the fuck is Sloane?" I demand.

The don pulls out a gun, points it at my chest and shoots. The impact throws me to my back.

It's everything I can do not to shift, but I resist the urge because right before he fired, I swear to fate, I heard one of Coach's lectures ricocheting through my brain.

Sometimes, in a fight, you gotta go down. Put your ego on

ice and let them think you're human like they are. Lose the personal fight. Take a win for the pack.

So I stay down where I fell, praying he won't come over and point that gun at my head to finish me.

One of his guys scurries over to grab the bag, and then they're gone. That fast.

Not sticking around to make sure I'm dead or get rid of my body, or anything.

Thank fuck.

I count to five, and then I'm up on my feet, tearing my clothes off and stuffing them behind a dumpster to shift. I need to be in wolf form to heal faster and stop the bleeding. And to get to that other address.

Please let her still be there.

Please let her still be alive.

I have zero hope they will let her go now that they have their shit. I have to find her.

Wolves should not be seen in cities in broad daylight, but I don't have time to worry about pack rules. All I can hope is that I'm moving fast enough that anyone who sees me will not be sure what they saw.

When I get to the location I'd memorized, I'm rewarded with her scent.

And then I see her.

She's being dragged to a running car by a slender blond guy with a gun to her ribs. There's a sack over her head, but she's walking on her own, and her hands are tied behind her back. I don't see anyone in the car.

So one guy. And a gun.

I can handle this. But I have to wait until that gun muzzle moves away from my female. The asshole opens the trunk and shoves her in. I wait until he shuts the trunk and walks around to the driver's side to let loose a snarl.

He does a double take when he sees me, lifts his gun to point, then changes his mind and opens the car door instead.

He's too late. My front paws land on his shoulders, and he's thrown back into the door. The gun falls to the ground. I have to hold back to keep from killing him—that instinct taking over so strongly it's hard to even think straight. But getting Sloane out of here is the priority.

And I have a getaway vehicle already running and waiting. So I sink my teeth into his shoulder as I knock him to the ground. Then I release him, making a show of growling and tearing his clothes like I'm rabid so he crab walks backward. A string of curses come out of his mouth in some language I don't understand. Not Italian. Maybe Russian.

I drive him further back, banking on the innate human fear of wolves to block any quick thinking on his part, and then I turn and launch myself into the driver's seat. I shift as I land—my fingers already stretched out to shut the door, my foot on the gas. I duck to keep him from seeing my face or shooting us and I take off, praying he won't have time to pick up his gun and fire into the trunk before we round the bend.

I whip through the wide industrial streets at ninety miles an hour. I don't see a tail, but I want to hide this car and get my girl out of the fucking trunk.

And get my clothes.

That thought makes me hang the next left and cruise right back to the place I got shot. I hide the car on the side of the warehouse and leap out.

"Sloane," I intone sharply, the second I hit the trunk opener and tumble out of the car.

"Bo?" Her voice is incredulous.

I yank the bag off her head and snap the zip tie around her wrists with one of my canines.

"Oh my God! I heard something, but I didn't know what the fuck was happening!" She scrambles up, and I get a look at her face, which sports a bruise the size of New Hampshire on one cheek.

I snarl, almost shifting again, and she flinches.

"Sorry," I give my head a hard shake, like it will shake the aggression right out of me. "Your face—fuck."

She throws her arms around my neck in a strangulating hold. I squeeze her, too, lifting her feet off the ground and burying my face in her hair. "Bo."

She's crying.

I squeeze tighter.

"I am madly in love with you." Her words whoosh inside me and fill every crack and crevice. She releases me. "You got shot. And we gotta get you some clothes."

"Right here." I grab my clothes from behind the dumpster and put them on.

"I'm sorry. I'm so sorry for everything." She's crying again.

I thumb away her tears, careful with the bruised side. "It's ok. It's okay, beautiful. You're mine now."

She blinks those reddish-brown eyes at me and leans in, laying her head softly against my chest. It's such a tender gesture. A soft, sweetness. So unlike what we've been with each other. I bookmark the moment because it feels like something important.

The first time she's really given herself to me. All of her.

I put my arm around her and lead her away from the warehouse. Away from the place I almost lost her. "Come on. I have to show you something."

~

Sloane

It's totally surreal. Bo and I are standing hand in hand across from my old middle school in front of an EZ storage. He filled me in on his fantastical part of the story on the walk. Don Salvatore has his money. He doesn't have me, but as far as he knows, someone kidnapped me from the trunk of a car following a wolf attack. He had already sold me to the Russian anyway, so I don't think he'll come looking for me again.

We figure we have a good chance of walking away from all this relatively unscathed.

"Your dad wrote to tell you if anything happened to you, to check a storage unit in here." Bo holds up my key ring—the one with the key to my bike lock. "The key was on here."

I shake my head. "Jesus. I had no idea."

He grins. "Yeah. Wanna see what else is in there?"

The corners of her lips turn up—she sees my excitement. "Definitely."

Bo unlocks the unit. "He put this in your name, only misspelled, so the Feds never found it to seize these assets. Smart man."

My heart's pounding. I'm guessing there's more money in there, based on Bo's excitement to show me. "What's in there?" I bounce on the balls of my feet like a child. I can't remember the last time I've been excited about anything. Not since my dad went to jail. But everything's cracked open now. The old Sloane has been busted apart in so many ways, and it hurt like hell, but now there's space. Space for the new me to emerge. Whoever she may be.

Bo shows me what he found. A couple more paintings and a box full of gold bars. More than two dozen of them. My breath tumbles out of me in a hysterical laugh. "So that's like...one and a half million dollars?"

"Yeah. Looks like your college is paid for, after all."

I cover my mouth with my hand. "Oh my God." My mind spins.

But my dad was a crook. He cheated people out of their money. Dammit—I can't keep it.

Bo bumps me with his hip. "You can fucking keep it," he says like he reads minds. "Some of his money had to be legit. At the very least, you should've gotten his life insurance policy, considering his suicide probably wasn't actually suicide."

"Well, I can sure think about it," I say. "What do we do with it now?"

Bo grins. "I have no idea. You might have to steal us a car to get home because I took a one-way flight here and have no wheels. Or maybe we could cash one of those in and buy you a car. Yeah—let's do that."

I throw myself at him again because it's all so fantastical and fun. The possibilities are wide open. He holds me close, and I press my cheek to his chest, listening to the steady sound of his heartbeat.

"Bo? You're not going to wipe my memories are you?"

His grip tightens on me. "Fuck, no. You're mine. I'll mark you if I have to prove it to them. No one's fucking taking you from me again."

I have no idea what that means, but I trust Bo.

If he says something, it's real.

He's keeping me.

It's such a strange, foreign feeling. All my life I've felt like an imposition. Apologized for my existence.

But now I've been claimed.

Bo wants me. He's keeping me.

And as much as I pushed him away, as terrified as I was to let anyone under my defenses, I can't resist him any more. Ever again.

Because he's mine, too.

My wolf boy. My hero. My knight.

EPILOGUE

THE CROWD in the parking lot after the game parts for me and the other alpha-holes. We just trounced Cave Hills, and I'm looking for Sloane. I saw her in the stands earlier, watching me, but I haven't touched her in days. Not since we got back from Michigan, and I hunger for her like a starved man.

"Hey Bo," Austin says. "You riding with me to the mesa?"

"Um, no, I'm good." I don't think I'm going to the mesa. I haven't even introduced Sloane to the animals of Wolf Ridge High. And I'm not sure I'm ready. Because if anyone's a dick to her—and there's a good chance they could be, considering she's from Cave Hills—I will fucking kill them. I also haven't told my buddies she knows what we are. That's a problem that still needs to be dealt with, although the alpha found out Bailey, Cole's girlfriend knows, and she hasn't been wiped. Of course she lives in Wolf Ridge, and her mom works at the brewery. Maybe they figure since she's part of the community, it's okay. Or maybe they'll wipe her when she graduates—I don't know.

Austin's little brother, Abe, steps closer, staring in the direction of the group of girls that includes Bailey. "I'm coming with you."

Austin scoffs. "The fuck you are." The mesa hangout is for the in-crowd. The senior alpha-holes and whoever else we determine deserves to be in our presence. And it's not usually underclassmen, even if they do play varsity.

I'm guessing Abe's sudden, bold interest is related to the other sophomore who's been hanging with our group because she came as a package deal with Bailey—the runt, Rayne. The shifter who can't shift.

Huh.

Wouldn't have expected that one. Nobody's paid that girl any interest since—ever. Funny how a newcomer can change someone's status overnight.

"Who are you looking for? Gone in Sixty Seconds?" Cole asks, noting my distraction.

"Shut up. Don't call her that."

"Is she here?" He follows my line of sight when the shock of recognition ripples through me. She's impossible to miss—her beautiful head stands above the rest of the Cave Hills crowd.

"Catch you guys later." I veer off in her direction.

I catch her waiting at her wheels. She bought a convertible BMW because the girl does have a penchant for a sweet ride. We traded a guy for a bar of gold in a private

Craigslist sale and drove back to Arizona with the top down and the radio blasting.

That was three days ago.

Three days since I've had my hands on her luscious body.

Three days since I've seen her in person.

Although she has been blowing up my phone. We've texted until late in the night every night since we got back. There's so much still to discover. To know about her.

But I still have the memory-wipe thing hanging over my head, and I have to figure out what to do.

I ignored Garrett's calls until he threatened to call his dad—Alpha Green—if he didn't hear from me. So I called and told him to fuck off.

Nicer than that, though, because I do want to keep my balls.

"Mark her or wipe her, those are your two options," he ordered. "I'm not having a random in Cave Hills exposing both packs."

So now I have a hard-on a mile long thinking about marking her, which is like getting married for a wolf. Only more. Because once a wolf has marked his mate—it's impossible to leave her. And I'm all in. I just have to make sure she is.

"Hey, Legs," I rumble, bumping her up against the Beamer and pinning her there with my hips, my arms caging her on either side.

She twines her arms around my neck and beams up at me. I feel every megawatt of that smile in my chest. She radiates joy. Openness. Connection. I thought she was beautiful before, and that was when her walls were up. When she projected the Cave Hills Princess vibe. Now, she's nothing short of breathtaking. Like a fucking goddess.

And she's all mine.

At least, I want her to be.

"Nice game, Muscles," she purrs. "So, tell me something—do you guys have to pretend to drop the ball and let yourselves get tackled sometimes, just to make it look real?"

"Shh." I make a show of looking around and grin. "Yeah. The game to us is to see how exciting we can make it before we lose. Or win."

"Mmm, fun." She squeezes my biceps and gives me bedroom eyes.

"Christ, Sloane. You keep looking at me like that, you're going to get fucked right up against this car," I growl.

"Is that the plan for tonight? You might still have to crawl in the window. Although Aunt Jen is crazy about you. You're her hero, too."

My hips jerk against hers, grinding my throbbing erection into her belly. "Stop getting me so hard. We actually have to talk."

She raises her brows. "Yeah?"

"Yeah, let's go for a drive." I open the driver's side.

Her lips purse into a smirk. "And I'm guessing you want to drive?"

I grin and lean in for a slow kiss. "Always." I pry the keys out of her hand while we mate mouths.

"Where are we going?"

"Let's just drive." I pull out of the mess of traffic and end up following my wolf's call up to the mountain. He wants her so bad, I'm already getting primed to mark her.

I pull off before we get to the mesa, where the Wolf Ridge kids like to build fires and drink beer on weekends. Then I turn off the car.

"Is this your version of Blueberry Hill?"

"Maybe. Listen, it's about what you know. What I got ordered to do."

She stiffens. "You can't wipe my memories, Bo."

I grab her hand and pull it to my chest. "I'm not. I won't. But here's the thing." I pause, realizing my heart is pounding. Does she feel it? I draw in a breath. "Wolves claim their mates. For life. There's a biology to it—a bite where we mark our mates' skin with our scent to keep other males away. If I mark you, they'll know you're safe."

Sloane gets very quiet. Barely breathing.

"So you *want* to bite me?"

My laugh tumbles out—a tension relief. "I'm *gonna* bite you, yeah." I say it like she has no choice, but of course I wouldn't claim her if she didn't agree. "And that means you're mine. Forever. Because I love you, Sloane. You're the fucking Earth and moon and stars to me. And I would die before I let you go. Even without a mating bite."

I scent the salt of tears before I realize she's crying.

"Sloane?" I'm slightly alarmed. Fuck. If she doesn't want this, we'll find another way.

"I love you, too," she chokes. "You're so much more than I ever expected or hoped for in a friend, boyfriend, lover—anything. And what scares me most is losing you. So, hell yes. I want you to bite me."

I'm on her in a second. The damn car is way too small for me, but I lunge across the center console and claim her mouth, licking between her lips, drinking from her. Just knowing she's consented has my canines descending, the serum for marking dripping sweetness on my tongue.

I can't lose control. I need to figure out how to do it without killing her—because claiming bites are usually deep and in the vicinity of the jugular. "Stay there," I growl and throw the door open, stalking around to her side. I drop to my knees in front of her open door and get my head between her knees. "Get those jeans down, beautiful. I need in."

She shimmies out of her jeans and panties, wrapping those long, gorgeous legs around my shoulders as I lick into her with the fervor of a fanatic. I'm a fanatic dedicated to pleasing my female. I work her into a frenzy, my swollen cock trapped against my fly the whole time, aching for release. But I'm not going to let it out. Not until I've taken care of the bite. I have to stay in control.

I screw one finger into her, my thumb rubbing her clit while I search for her G-spot.

When I find it, she screams, yanking on my hair. "Come for me, Legs," I growl, trailing my lips across her thigh toward the area of my target— the fleshy side of her ass, where scars won't show, and I won't endanger her. I insert a second finger and fuck her with them, hitting the raised tissue of her G-spot over and over again until she rolls and writhes and screams her release, her cunt squeezing and dripping around my fingers.

And then I sink my teeth into her.

My wolf roars with pleasure. I somehow manage not to jizz in my pants as I keep fucking and fucking her while extricating my teeth from her flesh and licking the wounds so they heal more quickly.

"Are you okay, beautiful? Tell me you're okay." The

scent of her blood has my wolf wild, even though he's the one who fucking did this to her. I'm in a frenzy—ready to kill for her. Ready to fuck. Ready to pledge my balls to her service for the rest of my life.

She pants, her slender fingers still wrapped in my hair. "I'm fine. It's fine."

I trail kisses down her leg. "I'm sorry I hurt you."

"I'm not. I freaking love it."

"I'll buy you a ring. Or whatever human thing you want," I promise, even though the only money I have is what's left from the fight. I can fight again. I'll provide for her if she doesn't want to use the rest of the gold.

Her laugh is low and sultry. "I don't need a ring, Bo Fenton. A bite is so much better. I got me a wolf."

The way she says *wolf* makes it sound like I'm some crazy, exotic creature. Which, I guess to her, I am.

I ease back and apply a big square adhesive bandage from the box I bought in preparation, then gently, gently help her back into her panties and jeans. I want to fuck her, but I'm gonna wait. Marking her took a huge edge off, so I can wait until she heals. Or until I sneak in her bedroom window after dropping her home.

"Where are all those cars going?" Sloane asks when another pair of headlights swing around the curve.

"To the mesa. You wanna meet the gang? The other alpha-holes and our royal court?" No one will mess with her now that I've marked her. There will be a shit-ton of gossip about it, but they'll learn to treat her like the queen she is.

She gives me that heart-stopping smile. "Definitely. Anything with you."

Anything with you.

Yeah. That pretty much sums it up. We have our whole lives in front of us—together. It can't get any better than that.

I lean in and kiss her on the lips. "I love you, Legs."

She makes a contented sound. "And I love you, Muscles."

I chuckle and shut the door, walking around to take her to meet my friends.

ACKNOWLEDGMENTS

I'm so incredibly grateful to Aubrey Cara, who loves the teen angst as much as I do and is willing to really deep dive into my books to help me make them so much better. Thank you to the members of Renee's Romper Room for your support and love (if you're not a member and you're on Facebook, please join!). Thanks to our ARC readers and to InkSlinger PR, Give Me Books PR and the bloggers who support my releases. You are all amazing!

WANT FREE RENEE ROSE BOOKS?

Go to http://subscribepage.com/alphastemp to sign up for Renee Rose's newsletter and receive free books. In addition to the free stories, you will also get special pricing, exclusive previews and news of new releases.

OTHER TITLES BY RENEE ROSE

Paranormal

Wolf Ridge High Series

Alpha Bully

Alpha Knight

Step Alpha

Alpha King

Bad Boy Alphas Series

Alpha's Temptation

Alpha's Danger

Alpha's Prize

Alpha's Challenge

Alpha's Obsession

Alpha's Desire

Alpha's War

Alpha's Mission

Alpha's Bane

Alpha's Secret

Alpha's Prey

Alpha's Sun

Shifter Ops

Alpha's Moon

Alpha's Vow

Alpha's Revenge

Alpha's Fire

Alpha's Rescue

Alpha's Command

Two Marks Series

Untamed

Tempted

Desired

Enticed

Wolf Ranch Series

Rough

Wild

Feral

Savage

Fierce

Ruthless

Midnight Doms

Alpha's Blood

His Captive Mortal

All Souls Night

Alpha Doms Series

The Alpha's Hunger

The Alpha's Promise

The Alpha's Punishment

The Alpha's Protection (Dirty Daddies)

Other Paranormal

The Winter Storm: An Ever After Chronicle

Contemporary

Chicago Sin

Den of Sins

Rooted in Sin

Made Men Series

Don't Tease Me

Don't Tempt Me

Don't Make Me

Chicago Bratva

"Prelude" in Black Light: Roulette War

The Director

The Fixer

"Owned" in Black Light: Roulette Rematch

The Enforcer

The Soldier

The Hacker

The Bookie

The Cleaner

The Player

The Gatekeeper

Alpha Mountain

Hero

Rebel

Warrior

Vegas Underground Mafia Romance

King of Diamonds

Mafia Daddy

Jack of Spades

Ace of Hearts

Joker's Wild

His Queen of Clubs

Dead Man's Hand

Wild Card

Daddy Rules Series

Fire Daddy

Hollywood Daddy

Stepbrother Daddy

Master Me Series

Her Royal Master

Her Russian Master

Her Marine Master

Yes, Doctor

Double Doms Series

Theirs to Punish

Theirs to Protect

Holiday Feel-Good

Scoring with Santa

Saved

Other Contemporary

Black Light: Valentine Roulette

Black Light: Roulette Redux

Black Light: Celebrity Roulette

Black Light: Roulette War

Black Light: Roulette Rematch

Punishing Portia (written as Darling Adams)

The Professor's Girl

Safe in his Arms

Sci-Fi

Zandian Masters Series

His Human Slave

His Human Prisoner

Training His Human

His Human Rebel

His Human Vessel

His Mate and Master

Zandian Pet

Their Zandian Mate

His Human Possession

Zandian Brides

Night of the Zandians

Bought by the Zandians

Mastered by the Zandians

Zandian Lights

Kept by the Zandian

Claimed by the Zandian

Stolen by the Zandian

Other Sci-Fi

The Hand of Vengeance

Her Alien Masters

ABOUT RENEE ROSE

USA TODAY BESTSELLING AUTHOR RENEE ROSE loves a dominant, dirty-talking alpha hero! She's sold over a million copies of steamy romance with varying levels of kink. Her books have been featured in USA Today's *Happily Ever After* and *Popsugar*. Named Eroticon USA's Next Top Erotic Author in 2013, she has also won *Spunky and Sassy's* Favorite Sci-Fi and Anthology author, *The Romance Reviews* Best Historical Romance, and *Spanking Romance Reviews'* Best Sci-fi, Paranormal, Historical, Erotic, Ageplay and favorite couple and author. She's hit the *USA Today* list five times with various anthologies.

Please follow her on:

Bookbub | Goodreads | Instagram | Tiktok

Renee loves to connect with readers!

www.reneeroseromance.com
reneeroseauthor@gmail.com

Click here to sign up for Renee Rose's newsletter and receive a free copy of *Theirs to Protect, Owned by the Marine, Theirs to Punish, The Alpha's Punishment, Disobedience at the Dressmaker's* and *Her Billionaire Boss*. In addition to the free stories, you will also get special pricing, exclusive previews and news of new releases.

Made in the USA
Monee, IL
20 January 2024

51529535R00143